all-time great classics

Three Men IN A BOAT

(A masterpiece of Jerome K. Jerome)

MANOJ PUBLICATIONS

Publishers :

MANOJ PUBLICATIONS

761, Main Road, Burari, Delhi-110084 (INDIA)

Mobile : 09999476076, 09868112194
08178823569, 08178854810

E-mail : info@manojpublications.com

For online shopping visit our website :
www.sawanonlinebookstore.com

From the Publisher's Desk

In this age of competition, none has the time to go through long novels which seem to have no endings. Maybe these kinds of novels were written during the time when people led leisurely life. They had plenty of time at their disposal. Reading good literary work on weekend was the main source of entertainment. Now the time has entirely changed. Readers search for short, excellent literary works which are comprised of well-designed illustrations. These illustrations clear their themes at very first glance. As a reader flips through the pages of an illustrated novel, each chapter unfolds in a very easy and interesting style.

Keeping this modern approach in mind, we have brought out this novel in a very novel way. Easy-to-understand language accompanied by life-like illustrations has added four-fold beauty to the novel. At the end of the novel, questions based on each and every chapter have been given to test the mental faculty of the reader.

All these outstanding features incorporated in this novel have made it suitable for young and old alike. Undoubtedly, it is ideal for classrooms, library and personal collection too.

About the Author

Jerome Klapka Jerome was born in Caldmore, Walsall, England, on 2nd may 1859. He was the fourth child of Jerome Clapp, an iron-monger and a lay preacher, who dabbled in architecture. Jerome K. Jerome had two sisters, Paulina and Blandina, and one brother, Milton, who died at an early age. The young Jerome wished to join politics but the death of both his parents in 1872, when he was 13 years old, forced him to quit his studies and find work to support himself and his two sisters. Inspired by his elder sister Blandina's love for the theatre, he joined the theatre but for a short tenure. With no evident success, he decided to become a journalist, writing essays, satires and short stories, but most of these were rejected. Over the next few years he remained a school teacher, a packer and a solicitor's clerk. Finally in 1885, he had some success with On the Stage- and Off, a humorous book whose publication opened the door for more plays and essays. In 1886, he penned down Idle Thoughts of an Idle Fellow, a collection of humorous essays. Then came the glorious moment when he penned down Three men in a Boat which was published in 1889. It became an instant success and has remained in print to date. Thereafter, he wrote a number of plays, essays and novels, but was never able to recapture the success of Three Men in a Boat. On 14th June 1927, he breathed his last after suffering a paralytic stroke and a cerebral haemorrhage.

Contents

Carl Hentschel

George Wingrave

Landlord

Montmorency The Dog

Chapter 1

Three Men Plan Their Journey

The narrator Jerome Klapka Jerome along with his two long time real-life friends – George Wingrave (who went on to become a senior manager in Barclays Bank) and Carl Hentschel (the founder of a London printing press) called Harris in the book, are spending an evening in the narrator's room. With them they have Montmorency, the dog, which is entirely fictional. In the room, they are smoking and discussing illnesses they fancy they suffer from. They conclude that they all are suffering from overwork and are in need of a holiday urgently. Both a stay in the countryside and a sea-trip are considered and then rejected. The narrator describes the bad experiences had by his brother –in-law and a friend on sea trips. Eventually, all the three men decide on a boating holiday, up River Thames, from Kingston upon the Thames to Oxford, during which they will camp, notwithstanding the narrator's anecdotes regarding previous mishaps with tents and camping stoves. In the pages to come Jerome K. Jerome (the narrator) himself narrates the events as they take place.

Harris said he felt such extraordinary fits of giddiness come over him at times, that he hardly knew what he was doing; and then George said that he had fits of giddiness too, and hardly knew what he was doing.

With me, it was my liver that was out of order. I knew it was my liver that was out of order, because I had just been reading a patent liver-pill circular, in which were detailed the various symptoms by which a man could tell when his liver was out of order. I had them all.

I sat for awhile, frozen with horror; and then, in the listlessness of despair, I again turned over the pages. I came to typhoid fever - read the symptoms - discovered that I had typhoid fever, must have had it for months without knowing it.

Then I wondered how long I had to live. I tried to examine myself. I felt my pulse. I could not at first feel any pulse at all. Then, all of a sudden, it seemed to start off. I pulled out my watch and timed it. I made it a hundred and forty-seven to the minute. I tried to feel my heart. I could not feel my heart. It had stopped beating. I have since been induced to come to the opinion that it must have been there all the time, and must have been beating, but I cannot account for it. I patted myself all over my front, from what I call my waist up to my head, and I went a bit round each side, and a little way up the back. But I could not feel or hear anything. I tried to look at my tongue. I stuck it out as far as ever it would go, and I shut one eye, and tried to examine it with the other. I could only see the tip, and the only thing that I could gain from that was to feel more certain than before that I had scarlet fever.

I had walked into that reading-room a happy, healthy man. I crawled out a decrepit wreck.

I went to my medical man. He is an old chum of mine, and feels my pulse, and looks at my tongue, and talks about the weather, all for nothing, when I fancy I'm ill; so I thought I would do him a good turn by going to him now. "What a doctor wants," I said, "is practice. He shall have me. He will get more practice out of me than out of seventeen hundred of your ordinary, commonplace patients, with only one or two diseases each." So I went straight up and saw him, and he said:

"Well, what's the matter with you?"

I said:

"I will not take up your time, dear boy, with telling you what is the matter with me. Life is brief, and you might pass away before I had finished. But I will tell you what is not the matter with me. I have not got housemaid's knee. Why I have not got housemaid's knee, I cannot tell you; but the fact remains that I have not got it. Everything else, however, I have got."

And I told him how I came to discover it all.

Then he opened me and looked down me, and clutched hold of my wrist, and then he hit me over the chest when I wasn't expecting it - a cowardly thing to do, I call it - and immediately afterwards butted me with the side of his head. After that, he sat down and wrote out a prescription, and folded it up and gave it me, and I put it in my pocket and went out.

I did not open it. I took it to the nearest chemist's, and handed it in. The man read it, and then handed it back.

He said he didn't keep it.

I said:

"You are a chemist?" He said:

"I am a chemist. If I was a co-operative stores and family hotel combined, I might be able to oblige you. Being only a chemist hampers me."

We sat there for half-an-hour, describing to each other our maladies. I explained to George and William

I objected to the sea trip strongly.

Harris how I felt when I got up in the morning, and William Harris told us how he felt when he went to bed; and George stood on the hearth-rug, and gave us a clever and powerful piece of acting, illustrative of how he felt in the night.

What it was that was actually the matter with us, we none of us could be sure of; but the unanimous opinion was that it - whatever it was - had been brought on by overwork.

"What we want is rest," said Harris.

"Rest and a complete change," said George. "The overstrain upon our brains has produced a general depression throughout the system. Change of scene, and absence of the necessity for thought, will restore the mental equilibrium."

I objected to the sea trip strongly. A sea trip does you good when you are going to have a couple of months of it, but, for a week, it is wicked.

I remember my brother-in-law going for a short sea trip once, for the benefit of his health. He took a return berth from London to Liverpool; and when he got to Liverpool, the only thing he was anxious about was to sell that return ticket.

It was offered round the town at a tremendous reduction, so I am told; and was eventually sold for eighteenpence to a bilious-looking youth who had just been advised by his medical men to go to the sea-side, and take exercise.

"Sea-side!" said my brother-in-law, pressing the ticket affectionately into his hand; "why, you'll have enough to last you a lifetime; and as for exercise! why, you'll get more exercise, sitting down on that ship, than you would turning somersaults on dry land."

He himself - my brother-in-law - came back by train. He said the North-Western Railway was healthy enough for him.

So I set my face against the sea trip. Not, as I explained, upon my own account. I was never queer. But I was afraid for George. George said he should be all right, and would rather like it, but he would advise Harris and me not to think of it, as he felt sure we should both be ill. Harris said that, to himself, it was always a mystery how people managed to get sick at sea - said he thought people must do it on purpose, from affectation - said he had often wished to be, but had never been able.

Then he told us the anecdotes of how he had gone across the Channel when it was so rough that the passengers had to be tied into their berths, and he and the captain were the only two living souls on board who were not ill. Sometimes it was he and the second mate who were not ill; but it was generally he and one other man. If not he and another man, then it was he by himself.

It is a curious fact, but nobody ever is sea-sick - on land. At sea, you come across plenty of people very bad indeed, whole boat-loads of them; but I never met a man yet, on land, who had ever known at all what it was to be sea-sick. Where the thousands upon thousands of bad sailors that swarm in every ship hide themselves when they are on land is a mystery.

For myself, I have discovered an excellent preventive against sea-sickness, in balancing myself. You stand in the centre of the deck, and, as the ship heaves and pitches, you move your body about, so as to keep it always straight. When the front of the ship rises, you lean forward, till the deck almost touches your nose; and when its back end gets up, you lean backwards. This is all very well for an hour or two; but you can't balance yourself for a week.

George said, "Let's go up the river."

He said we should have fresh air, exercise and quiet; the constant change of scene would occupy our minds (including what there was of Harris's); and the hard work would give us a good appetite, and make us sleep well.

The only one who was not struck with the suggestion was Montmorency, the dog. He never did care for the river.

"It's all very well for you fellows," he says; "you like it, but I don't. There's nothing for me to do. Scenery is not in my line, and I don't smoke. If I see a rat, you won't stop; and if I go to sleep, you get fooling about with the boat, and slop me overboard. If you ask me, I call the whole thing bally foolishness."

We were three to one, however, and the motion was carried.

We pulled out the maps, and discussed plans.

We arranged to start on the following Saturday from Kingston. Harris and I would go down in the morning, and take the boat up to Chertsey, and George, who would not be able to get away from the City till the afternoon (George goes to sleep at a bank from ten to four each day, except Saturdays, when they wake him up and put him outside at two), would meet us there.

Should we "camp out" or sleep at inns?

George and I were for camping out. We said it would be so wild and free, so patriarchal like.

Then we run our little boat into some quiet nook, and the tent is pitched, and the frugal supper cooked and eaten. Then the big pipes are filled and lighted, and the pleasant chat goes round in musical undertone; while, in the pauses of our talk, the river, playing round the boat, prattles strange old tales and secrets, sings low the old child's song that it has sung so many thousand years - will sing so many thousand years to come, before its voice grows harsh and old - a song that we, who have learnt to love its changing face, who have so often nestled on its yielding bosom, think, somehow, we understand, though we could not tell you in mere words the story that we listen to.

Harris said: "How about when it rained?"

You can never rouse Harris. There is no poetry about Harris - no wild yearning for the unattainable. Harris never "weeps, he knows not why." If Harris's eyes fill with tears, you can bet it is because Harris has been eating raw onions, or has put too much Worcester over his chop.

If you were to stand at night by the sea-shore with Harris, and say:

"Hark! do you not hear? Is it but the mermaids singing deep below the waving waters; or sad spirits, chanting dirges for white corpses, held by seaweed?" Harris would take you by the arm, and say:

"I know what it is, old man; you've got a chill. Now, you come along with me. I know a place round the corner here, where you can get a drop of the finest Scotch whisky you ever tasted - put you right in less than no time."

Harris always does know a place round the corner where you can get something brilliant in the drinking line. I believe that if you met Harris up in Paradise (supposing such a thing likely), he would immediately greet you with:

"So glad you've come, old fellow; I've found a nice place round the corner here, where you can get some really first-class nectar."

In the morning you are all three speechless, owing to having caught severe colds in the night; you also feel very quarrelsome, and you swear at each other in hoarse whispers during the whole of breakfast time.

We therefore decided that we would sleep out on fine nights; and hotel it, and inn it, and pub it, like respectable folks, when it was wet, or when we felt inclined for a change.

Montmorency hailed this compromise with much approval. He does not revel in romantic solitude. Give him something noisy; and if a trifle low, so much the jollier. To look at Montmorency you would imagine that he was an angel sent upon the earth, for some reason withheld from mankind, in the shape of a small fox-terrier.

When first he came to live at my expense, I never thought I should be able to get him to stop long. I used to sit down and look at him, as he sat on the rug and looked up at me, and think: "Oh, that dog will never live. He will be snatched up to the bright skies in a chariot, that is what will happen to him."

Having thus settled the sleeping arrangements to the satisfaction of all four of us, the only thing left to discuss was what we should take with us; and this we had begun to argue, when Harris said he'd had enough oratory for one night, and proposed that we should go out and have a smile, saying that he had found a place, round by the square, where you could really get a drop of Irish worth drinking.

George said he felt thirsty (I never knew George when he didn't); and, as I had a presentiment that a little whisky, warm, with a slice of lemon, would do my complaint good, the debate was, by common assent, adjourned to the following night; and the assembly put on its hats and went out.

❐

Chapter 2

Discussing the Things

So, on the following evening, we again assembled, to discuss and arrange our plans. Harris said:

"Now, the first thing to settle is what to take with us. Now, you get a bit of paper and write down, J., and you get the grocery catalogue, George, and somebody give me a bit of pencil, and then I'll make out a list."

That's Harris all over - so ready to take the burden of everything himself, and put it on the backs of other people.

He always reminds me of my poor Uncle Podger. You never saw such a commotion up and down a house, in all your life, as when my Uncle Podger undertook to do a job. A picture would have come home from the frame-maker's, and be standing in the dining-room, waiting to be put up; and Aunt Podger would ask what was to be done with it, and Uncle Podger would say:

"Oh, you leave that to me. Don't you, any of you, worry yourselves about that? I'll do all that."

Harris will be just that sort of man when he grows up, I know, and I told him so. I said I could not permit him to take so much labour upon himself. I said:

"No; *you* get the paper, and the pencil, and the catalogue, and George write down, and I'll do the work."

The first list we made out had to be discarded. It was clear that the upper reaches of the Thames would not allow of the navigation of a boat sufficiently large to take the things we had set down as indispensable; so we tore the list up, and looked at one another!

George said:

"You know we are on a wrong track altogether. We must not think of the things we could do with, but only of the things that we can't do without."

"We won't take a tent, suggested George; "we will have a boat with a cover. It is ever so much simpler, and more comfortable."

It seemed a good thought, and we adopted it. I do not know whether you have ever seen the thing I mean. You fix iron hoops up over the boat, and stretch a huge canvas over them, and fasten it down all round, from stem to stern, and it converts the boat into a sort of little house, and it is beautifully cosy, though a trifle stuffy; but there, everything has its drawbacks, as the man said when his mother-in-law died, and they came down upon him for the funeral expenses.

George said that in that case we must take a rug each, a lamp, some soap, a brush and comb (between us), a toothbrush (each), a basin, some tooth-powder, some shaving tackle (sounds like a French exercise, doesn't it?), and a couple of big-towels for bathing. I notice that people always make gigantic arrangements for bathing when they are going anywhere near the water, but that they don't bathe much when they are there.

I urged upon George, however, how much pleasanter it would be to have Harris clean and fresh about the boat, even if we did have to take a few more hundredweight of provisions; and he got to see it in my light, and withdrew his opposition to Harris's bath.

Agreed, finally, that we should take three bath towels, so as not to keep each other waiting.

For clothes, George said two suits of flannel would be sufficient, as we could wash them ourselves, in the river, when they got dirty. We asked him if he had ever tried washing flannels in the river, and he replied: "No, not exactly himself like; but he knew some fellows who had, and it was easy enough;" and Harris and I were weak enough to fancy he knew what he was talking about, and that three respectable young men, without position or influence, and with no experience in washing, could really clean their own shirts and trousers in the river Thames with a bit of soap.

We were to learn in the days to come, when it was too late, that George was a miserable impostor, who could evidently have known nothing whatever about the matter. If you had seen these clothes after - but, as the shilling shockers say, we anticipate.

George impressed upon us to take a change of under-things and plenty of socks, in case we got upset and wanted a change; also plenty of handkerchiefs, as they would do to wipe things, and a pair of leather boots as well as our boating shoes, as we should want them if we got upset.

Then we discussed the food question. George said: "Begin with breakfast." (George is so practical.) "Now for breakfast we shall want a frying-pan" - (Harris said it was indigestible; but we merely urged him not to be an ass, and George went on) - "a tea-pot and a kettle, and a methylated spirit stove."

"No oil," said George, with a significant look.

"No oil," said George, with a significant look; and Harris and I agreed.

So, we confined ourselves to methylated spirit. Even that is bad enough. You get methylated pie and methylated cake. But methylated spirit is more wholesome when taken into the system in large quantities than paraffine oil.

For other breakfast things, George suggested eggs and bacon, which were easy to cook, cold meat, tea, bread and butter, and jam. For lunch, he said, we could have biscuits, cold meat, bread and butter, and jam - but *no cheese*. Cheese, like oil, makes too much of itself. It wants the whole boat to itself. It goes through the hamper, and gives a cheesy flavour to everything else there. You can't tell whether you are eating apple-pie or German sausage, or strawberries and cream. It all seems cheese. There is too much odour about cheese.

Fond as I am of cheese, therefore, I hold that George was right in declining to take any.

"We shan't want any tea," said George (Harris's face fell at this); "but we'll have a good round, square, slap-up meal at seven - dinner, tea, and supper combined."

Harris grew more cheerful. George suggested meat and fruit pies, cold meat, tomatoes, fruit, and green stuff. For drink, we took some wonderful sticky concoction of Harris's, which you mixed with water and called lemonade, plenty of tea, and a bottle of whisky, in case, as George said, we got upset.

It seemed to me that George harped too much on the getting-upset idea. It seemed to me the wrong spirit to go about the trip in.

But I'm glad we took the whisky.

We didn't take beer or wine. They are a mistake up the river. They make you feel sleepy and heavy. A glass in the evening when you are wandering aimlessly round the town and looking at the girls is all right enough; but don't drink when the sun is blazing down on your head, and you've got hard work to do.

We made a list of the things to be taken, and a pretty lengthy one it was, before we parted that evening. The next day, which was Friday, we got them all together, and met in the evening to pack. We got a big Gladstone for the clothes, and a couple of hampers for the victuals and the cooking utensils. We moved the table up against the window, piled everything in a heap in the middle of the floor, and sat round and looked at it.

I said I'd pack.

I rather pride myself on my packing. Packing is one of those many things that I feel I know more about than any other person living. (It surprises me myself, sometimes, how many of these subjects there are.) I impressed the fact upon George and Harris, and told them that they had better leave the whole matter entirely to me. They fell into the suggestion with a readiness that had something uncanny about it. George put on a pipe and spread himself over the easy-chair, and Harris cocked his legs on the table and lit a cigar.

This was hardly what I intended. What I had meant, of course, was, that I should boss the job, and that Harris and George should potter about under my directions, I pushing them aside every now and then with, "Oh, you - !" "Here, let me do it." "There you are, simple enough!" - really teaching them, as you might say. Their taking it in the way they did irritated me. There is nothing does irritate me more than seeing other people sitting about doing nothing when I'm working.

I lived with a man once who used to make me mad that way. He would loll on the sofa and watch me doing things by the hour together, following me round the room with his eyes, wherever I went. He said it did him real good to look on at me, messing about. He said it made him feel that life was not an idle dream to be gaped and yawned through, but a noble task, full of duty and stern work. He said he often wondered now how he could have gone on before he met me, never having anybody to look at while they worked.

Now, I'm not like that. I can't sit still and see another man slaving and working. I want to get up and superintend, and walk round with my hands in my pockets, and tell him what to do. It is my energetic nature. I can't help it.

However, I did not say anything, but started the packing. It seemed a longer job than I had thought it was going to be; but I got the bag finished at last, and I sat on it and strapped it.

"Ain't you going to put the boots in?" said Harris.

And I looked round, and found I had forgotten them. That's just like Harris. He couldn't have said a word until I'd got the bag shut and strapped, of course. And George laughed - one of those irritating, senseless, chuckle-headed, crack-jawed laughs of his. They do make me so wild.

I opened the bag and packed the boots in; and then, just as I was going to close it, a horrible idea occurred to me. Had I packed my tooth-brush? I don't know how it is, but I never do know whether I've packed my tooth-brush.

My tooth-brush is a thing that haunts me when I'm travelling, and makes my life a misery. I dream that I haven't packed it, and wake up in a cold perspiration, and get out of bed and hunt for it. And, in the morning, I pack it before I have used it, and have to unpack again to get it, and it is always the last thing I turn out of the bag; and then I repack and forget it, and have to rush upstairs for it at the last moment and carry it to the railway station, wrapped up in my pocket-handkerchief.

Of course I had to turn every mortal thing out now, and, of course, I could not find it. I rummaged the things up into much the same state that they must have been before the world was created, and when chaos reigned. Of course, I found George's and Harris's eighteen times over, but I couldn't find my own. I put the things back one by one, and held everything up and shook it. Then I found it inside a boot. I repacked once more.

When I had finished, George asked if the soap was in. I said I didn't care a hang whether the soap was in or whether it wasn't; and I slammed the bag to and strapped it, and found that I had packed my tobacco-pouch in it, and had to re-open it. It got shut up finally at 10.5 p.m., and then there remained the hampers to do. Harris said that we should be wanting to start in less than twelve hours' time, and thought that he and George had better do the rest; and I agreed and sat down, and they had a go.

They began in a light-hearted spirit, evidently intending to show me how to do it. I made no comment; I only waited. When George is hanged, Harris will be the worst packer in this world; and I looked at the piles of plates and cups, and kettles, and bottles and jars, and pies, and stoves, and cakes, and tomatoes, &c., and felt that the thing would soon become exciting.

It did. They started with breaking a cup. That was the first thing they did. They did that just to show you what they *could* do, and to get you interested.

Then Harris packed the strawberry jam on top of a tomato and squashed it, and they had to pick out the tomato with a teaspoon.

And then it was George's turn, and he trod on the butter. I didn't say anything, but I came over and sat on the edge of the table and watched them. It irritated them more than anything I could have said. I felt that. It made them nervous and excited, and they stepped on things, and put things behind them, and then couldn't find them when they wanted them; and they packed the pies at the bottom, and put heavy things on top, and smashed the pies in.

They upset salt over everything, and as for the butter! I never saw two men do more with one-and-twopence worth of butter in my whole life than they did. After George had got it off his slipper, they tried to put it in the kettle. It wouldn't go in, and what *was* in wouldn't come out. They did scrape it out at last, and put it down on a chair, and Harris sat on it, and it stuck to him, and they went looking for it all over the room.

"I'll take my oath I put it down on that chair," said George, staring at the empty seat.

"I saw you do it myself, not a minute ago," said Harris.

Then they started round the room again looking for it; and then they met again in the centre, and stared at one another.

"Most extraordinary thing I ever heard of," said George.

"So mysterious!" said Harris.

Then George got round at the back of Harris and saw it.

"Why, here it is all the time," he exclaimed, indignantly.

"Where?" cried Harris, spinning round.

"Stand still, can't you!" roared George, flying after him.

And they got it off, and packed it in the teapot.

Montmorency was in it all, of course. Montmorency's ambition in life, is to get in the way and be sworn at. If he can squirm in anywhere where he particularly is not wanted, and be a perfect nuisance, and make people mad, and have things thrown at his head, then he feels his day has not been wasted.

To get somebody to stumble over him, and curse him steadily for an hour, is his highest aim and object; and, when he has succeeded in accomplishing this, his conceit becomes quite unbearable.

He came and sat down on things, just when they were wanted to be packed; and he laboured under the fixed belief that, whenever Harris or George reached out their hand for anything, it was his cold, damp nose that they wanted. He put his leg into the jam, and he worried the teaspoons, and he pretended that the lemons were rats, and got into the hamper and killed three of them before Harris could land him with the frying-pan.

Harris said I encouraged him. I didn't encourage him. A dog like that don't want any encouragement.

It's the natural, original sin that is born in him that makes him do things like that.

The packing was done at 12.50; and Harris sat on the big hamper, and said he hoped nothing would be found broken. George said that if anything was broken it was broken, which reflection seemed to comfort him. He also said he was ready for bed.

We were all ready for bed. Harris was to sleep with us that night, and we went upstairs.

We tossed for beds, and Harris had to sleep with me. He said:

"Do you prefer the inside or the outside, J.?"

I said I generally preferred to sleep *inside* a bed.

Harris said it was old.

George said:

"What time shall I wake you fellows?"

Harris said: "Seven."

I said:

"No - six," because I wanted to write some letters.

Harris and I had a bit of a row over it, but at last split the difference, and said half-past six.

"Wake us at 6.30, George," we said.

George made no answer, and we found, on going over, that he had been asleep for some time; so we placed the bath where he could tumble into it on getting out in the morning, and went to bed ourselves. ❐

Chapter 3

On Their Way

It was Mrs. Poppets that woke me up next morning. She said:

"Do you know that it's nearly nine o'clock, sir?"

"Nine o' what?" I cried, starting up.

"Nine o'clock," she replied, through the keyhole. "I thought you was a-oversleeping yourselves."

I woke Harris, and told him. He said: "I thought you wanted to get up at six?"

"So I did," I answered; "why didn't you wake me?"

"How could I wake you, when you didn't wake me?" he retorted. "Now we shan't get on the water till after twelve. I wonder you take the trouble to get up at all."

"Um," I replied, "lucky for you that I do. If I hadn't woke you, you'd have lain there for the whole fortnight."

We snarled at one another in this strain for the next few minutes, when we were interrupted by a defiant snore from George.

It reminded us, for the first time since our being called, of his existence.

There he laid—the man who had wanted to know what time he should wake us - on his back, with his mouth wide open, and his knees stuck up.

I don't know why it should be, I am sure; but the sight of another man asleep in bed when I am up, maddens me. It seems to me so shocking to see the precious hours of a man's life - the priceless moments that will never come back to him again - being wasted in mere brutish sleep.

There was George, throwing away in hideous sloth the inestimable gift of time; his valuable life, every second of which he would have to account for hereafter, passing away from him, unused. He might have been up stuffing himself with eggs and bacon, irritating the dog, or flirting with the servant instead of sprawling there, sunk in soul-clogging oblivion.

It was a terrible thought. Harris and I appeared to be struck by it at the same instant. We determined to save him, and, in this noble resolve, our own dispute was forgotten. We flew across and slung the clothes off him, and Harris landed him one with a slipper, and I shouted in his ear, and he awoke.

"Wasermarrer?" he observed, sitting up.

"Get up, you fat-headed chunk!" roared Harris. "It's quarter to ten."

"What!" he shrieked, jumping out of bed into the bath; "Who the thunder put this thing here?"

We told him he must have been a fool not to see the bath.

We finished dressing, and, when it came to the extras, we remembered that we had packed the tooth-brushes and the brush and comb (that tooth-brush of mine will be the death of me, I know), and we had to go downstairs, and fish them out of the bag. And when we had done that George wanted the shaving tackle. We told him that he would have to go without shaving

We went downstairs to breakfast.

that morning, as we weren't going to unpack that bag again for him, nor for anyone like him.

He said:

"Don't be absurd. How can I go into the City like this?"

It was certainly rather rough on the City, but what cared we for human suffering? As Harris said, in his common, vulgar way, the City would have to lump it.

We went downstairs to breakfast. Montmorency had invited two other dogs to come and see him off, and they were whiling away the time by fighting on the doorstep. We calmed them with an umbrella, and sat down to chops and cold beef.

Then Harris and I, having finished up the few things left on the table, carted out our luggage on to the doorstep, and waited for a cab.

There seemed a good deal of luggage, when we put it all together. There was the Gladstone and the small hand-bag, and the two hampers, and a large roll of rugs, and some four or five overcoats and macintoshes, and a few umbrellas, and then there was a melon by itself in a bag, because it was too bulky to go in anywhere, and a couple of pounds of grapes in another bag, and a Japanese paper umbrella, and a frying pan, which, being too long to pack, we had wrapped round with brown paper.

It did look a lot, and Harris and I began to feel rather ashamed of it, though why we should be, I can't see. No cab came by, but the street boys did, and got interested in the show, apparently, and stopped.

Biggs's boy was the first to come round. Biggs is our greengrocer, and his chief talent lies in securing the services of the most abandoned and unprincipled errand-boys that civilisation has as yet produced. If anything more than usually villainous in the boy-line crops up in our neighbourhood, we know that it is Biggs's latest. I was told that, at the time of the Great Coram Street murder, it was promptly concluded by our street that Biggs's boy (for that period) was at the bottom of it, and had he not been able, in reply to the severe cross-examination to which he was subjected by No. 19, when he called there for orders the morning after the crime (assisted by No. 21, who happened to be on the step at the time), to prove a complete *alibi*, it would have gone hard with him. I didn't know Biggs's boy at that time, but, from what I have seen of them since, I should not have attached much importance to that *alibi* myself.

At last, an empty cab turned up (it is a street where, as a rule, and when they are not wanted, empty cabs pass at the rate of three a minute, and hang about, and get in your way), and packing ourselves and our belongings into it, and shooting out a couple of Montmorency's friends, who had evidently sworn never to forsake him, we drove away amidst the cheers of the crowd, Biggs's boy shying a carrot after us for luck.

We got to Waterloo at eleven, and asked where the eleven-five started from. Of course nobody knew; nobody at Waterloo ever does know where a train is going to start from, or where a train when it does start is going to, or anything about it. The porter who took our things thought it would go from number two platform, while another porter, with whom he discussed the question, had heard a rumour that it would go from number one. The station-master, on the other hand, was convinced it would start from the local.

To put an end to the matter, we went upstairs, and asked the traffic superintendent, and he told us that he had just met a man, who said he had seen it at number three platform. We went to number three platform, but the authorities there said that they rather thought that train was the Southampton express, or else the Windsor loop. But they were sure it wasn't the Kingston train, though why they were sure it wasn't they couldn't say.

Then our porter said he thought that must be it on the high-level platform; said he thought he knew the train. So we went to the high-level platform, and saw the engine-driver, and asked him if he was going to Kingston. He said he couldn't say for certain of course, but that he rather thought he was. Anyhow, if he wasn't the 11.5 for Kingston, he said he was pretty confident he was the 9.32 for Virginia Water, or the 10 a.m. express for the Isle of Wight, or somewhere in that direction, and we should all know when we got there. We slipped half-a-crown into his hand, and begged him to be the 11.5 for Kingston.

"Nobody will ever know, on this line," we said, "what you are, or where you're going. You know the way, you slip off quietly and go to Kingston."

"Well, I don't know, gents," replied the noble fellow, "but I suppose some train's got to go to Kingston; and I'll do it. Gimme the half-crown."

Thus we got to Kingston by the London and South-Western Railway.

We learnt, afterwards, that the train we had come by was really the Exeter mail, and that they had spent hours at Waterloo, looking for it, and nobody knew what had become of it.

Our boat was waiting for us at Kingston just below

bridge, and to it we wended our way, and round it we stored our luggage, and into it we stepped.

"Are you all right, sir?" said the man.

"Right it is," we answered; and with Harris at the sculls and I at the tiller-lines, and Montmorency, unhappy and deeply suspicious, in the prow, out we shot on to the waters which, for a fortnight, were to be our home.

The quaint back streets of Kingston, where they came down to the water's edge, looked quite picturesque in the flashing sunlight, the glinting river with its drifting barges, the wooded towpath, the trim-kept villas on the other side, Harris, in a red and orange blazer, grunting away at the sculls, the distant glimpses of the grey old palace of the Tudors, all made a sunny picture, so bright but calm, so full of life, and yet so peaceful, that, early in the day though it was, I felt myself being dreamily lulled off into a musing fit.

But, there, I don't suppose I should really care for it when it came to actual practice. It would be so ghastly dull and depressing in the evening, when your lamp cast uncanny shadows on the panelled walls, and the echo of distant feet rang through the cold stone corridors, and now drew nearer, and now died away, and all was death-like silence, save the beating of one's own heart.

We are the creatures of the sun, we men and women. We love light and life. That is why we crowd into the towns and cities, and the country grows more and more deserted every year. In the sunlight - in the daytime, when Nature is alive and busy all around us, we like the open hill-sides and the deep woods well enough: but in the night, when our Mother Earth has gone to sleep, and left us waking, oh! the world seems so lonesome, and we get frightened, like children in a silent house. Then we sit and sob, and long for the gas-lit streets, and the sound of human voices, and the answering throb of human life. We feel so helpless and so little in the great stillness, when the dark trees rustle in the night-wind. There are so many ghosts about, and their silent sighs make us feel so sad. Let us gather together in the great cities, and light huge bonfires of a million gas-jets, and shout and sing together, and feel brave.

Harris asked me if I'd ever been in the maze at Hampton Court. He said he went in once to show somebody else the way. He had studied it up in a map, and it was so simple that it seemed foolish - hardly worth the two pence charged for admission. Harris said he thought that map must have been got up as a practical joke, because it wasn't a bit like the real thing, and only misleading. It was a country cousin that Harris took in. He said:

"We'll just go in here, so that you can say you've been, but it's very simple. It's absurd to call it a maze. You keep on taking the first turning to the right. We'll just walk round for ten minutes, and then go and get some lunch."

They met some people soon after they had got inside, who said they had been there for three-quarters of an hour, and had had about enough of it. Harris told them they could follow him, if they liked; he was just going in, and then should turn round and come out again. They said it was very kind of him, and fell behind, and followed.

They picked up various other people who wanted to

get it over, as they went along, until they had absorbed all the persons in the maze. People who had given up all hopes of ever getting either in or out, or of ever seeing their home and friends again, plucked up courage at the sight of Harris and his party, and joined the procession, blessing him. Harris said he should judge there must have been twenty people, following him, in all; and one woman with a baby, who had been there all the morning, insisted on taking his arm, for fear of losing him.

Harris kept on turning to the right, but it seemed a long way, and his cousin said he supposed it was a very big maze.

"Oh, one of the largest in Europe," said Harris.

"Yes, it must be," replied the cousin, "because we've walked a good two miles already."

Harris began to think it rather strange himself, but he held on until, at last, they passed the half of a penny bun on the ground that Harris's cousin swore he had noticed there seven minutes ago. Harris said: "Oh, impossible!" but the woman with the baby said, "Not at all," as she herself had taken it from the child, and thrown it down there, just before she met Harris. She also added that she wished she never had met Harris, and expressed an opinion that he was an impostor. That made Harris mad, and he produced his map, and explained his theory.

"The map may be all right enough," said one of the party, "if you know whereabouts in it we are now."

Harris didn't know, and suggested that the best thing to do would be to go back to the entrance, and begin again. For the beginning again part of it there was not much enthusiasm; but with regard to the advisability of going back to the entrance there was complete unanimity, and so they turned, and trailed after Harris again, in the opposite direction. About ten minutes more passed, and then they found themselves in the centre.

Harris thought at first of pretending that that was what he had been aiming at; but the crowd looked dangerous, and he decided to treat it as an accident.

Anyhow, they had got something to start from then. They did know where they were, and the map was once more consulted, and the thing seemed simpler than ever, and off they started for the third time.

And three minutes later they were back in the centre again.

After that, they simply couldn't get anywhere else. Whatever way they turned brought them back to the middle. It became so regular at length, that some of the people stopped there, and waited for the others to take a walk round, and come back to them. Harris drew out his map again, after a while, but the sight of it only infuriated the mob, and they told him to go and curl his hair with it. Harris said that he couldn't help feeling that, to a certain extent, he had become unpopular.

They all got crazy at last, and sang out for the keeper, and the man came and climbed up the ladder outside, and shouted out directions to them. But all their heads were, by this time, in such a confused whirl that they were incapable of grasping anything, and so the man told them to stop where they were, and he would come to them. They huddled together, and waited; and he climbed down, and came in.

He was a young keeper, as luck would have it, and

new to the business; and when he got in, he couldn't find them, and he wandered about, trying to get to them, and then HE got lost. They caught sight of him, every now and then, rushing about the other side of the hedge, and he would see them, and rush to get to them, and they would wait there for about five minutes, and then he would reappear again in exactly the same spot, and ask them where they had been.

They had to wait till one of the old keepers came back from his dinner before they got out.

Harris said he thought it was a very fine maze, so far as he was a judge; and we agreed that we would try to get George to go into it, on our way back.

❒

Chapter 4

At the River-bank

It was while passing through Moulsey Lock an enclosure (as in a canal) with gates at each end, used in raising or lowering boats as they pass from level to level. that Harris told me about his maze experience. It took us some time to pass through, as we were the only boat, and it is a big lock. I don't think I ever remember to have seen Moulsey Lock, before, with only one boat in it. It is, I suppose, Boulter's not even excepted, the busiest lock on the river.

I have stood and watched it, sometimes, when you could not see any water at all, but only a brilliant tangle of bright blazers, and gay caps, and saucy hats, and many-coloured parasols, and silken rugs, and cloaks, and streaming ribbons, and dainty whites; when looking down into the lock from the quay, you might fancy it was a huge box into which flowers of every hue and shade had been thrown pell-mell, and lay piled up in a rainbow heap, that covered every corner.

On a fine Sunday it presents this appearance nearly all day long, while, up the stream, and down the stream, lie, waiting their turn, outside the gates, long lines of still more boats; and boats are drawing near and passing away, so that the sunny river, from the Palace up to Hampton Church, is dotted and decked with yellow, and blue, and orange, and white, and red, and pink. All the inhabitants of Hampton and Moulsey dress themselves up in boating costume, and come and loiter round the lock with their dogs, and flirt, and smoke, and watch the boats; and, altogether, what with the caps and jackets of the men, the pretty coloured dresses of the women, the excited dogs, the moving boats, the white sails, the pleasant landscape, and the sparkling water, it is one of the gayest sights I know of near this dull old London town.

Harris always keeps to shades or mixtures of orange or yellow, but I don't think he is at all wise in this. His complexion is too dark for yellows. Yellows don't suit him: there can be no question about it. I want him to take to blue as a background, with white or cream for relief; but, there! the less taste a person has in dress, the more obstinate he always seems to be. It is a great pity, because he will never be a success as it is, while there are one or two colours in which he might not really look so bad, with his hat on.

George has bought some new things for this trip, and I'm rather vexed about them. The blazer is loud. I should not like George to know that I thought so, but there really is no other word for it. He brought it home and showed it to us on Thursday evening. We asked him what colour he called it, and he said he didn't know. He didn't think there was a name for the colour. The man had told him it was an Oriental design. George put it on, and asked us what we thought of it. Harris said that, as an object to hang over a flower-bed in early spring to frighten the birds away, he should respect it; but that, considered as an article of dress for any human being, except a Margate nigger, it made him ill. George got quite huffy; but, as Harris said, if he didn't want his opinion, why did he ask for it?

What troubles Harris and myself, with regard to it, is that we are afraid it will attract attention to the boat.

Girls, also, don't look half bad in a boat, if prettily dressed. Nothing is more fetching, to my thinking, than a tasteful boating costume. But a "boating costume," it would be as well if all ladies would understand, ought to be a costume that can be worn in a boat, and not merely under a glass-case. It utterly spoils an excursion if you have folk in the boat who are thinking all the time a good deal more of their dress than of the trip. It was my misfortune once to go for a water picnic with two ladies of this kind. We did have a lively time!

They were both beautifully got up - all lace and silky stuff, and flowers, and ribbons, and dainty shoes, and light gloves. But they were dressed for a photographic studio, not for a river picnic. They were the "boating costumes" of a French fashion-plate. It was ridiculous, fooling about in them anywhere near real earth, air, and water.

The first thing was that they thought the boat was not clean. We dusted all the seats for them, and then assured them that it was, but they didn't believe us. One of them rubbed the cushion with the forefinger of her glove, and showed the result to the other, and they both sighed, and sat down, with the air of early Christian martyrs trying to make themselves comfortable up against the stake. You are liable to occasionally splash a little when sculling, and it appeared that a drop of water ruined those costumes. The mark never came out, and a stain was left on the dress for ever.

I was stroke. I did my best. I feathered some two feet

The girls huddled up close together.

high, and I paused at the end of each stroke to let the blades drip before returning them, and I picked out a smooth bit of water to drop them into again each time. (Bow said, after a while, that he did not feel himself a sufficiently accomplished oarsman to pull with me, but that he would sit still, if I would allow him, and study my stroke. He said it interested him.) But, notwithstanding all this, and try as I would, I could not help an occasional flicker of water from going over those dresses.

The girls did not complain, but they huddled up close together, and set their lips firm, and every time a drop touched them, they visibly shrank and shuddered. It was a noble sight to see them suffering thus in silence, but it unnerved me altogether. I am too sensitive. I got wild and fitful in my rowing, and splashed more and more, the harder I tried not to.

I gave it up at last; I said I'd row bow. Bow thought the arrangement would be better too, and we changed places. The ladies gave an involuntary sigh of relief when they saw me go, and quite brightened up for a moment. Poor girls! they had better have put up with me. The man they had got now was a jolly, light-hearted, thick-headed sort of a chap, with about as much sensitiveness in him as there might be in a Newfoundland puppy. You might look daggers at him for an hour and he would not notice it, and it would not trouble him if he did. He set a good, rollicking, dashing stroke that sent the spray playing all over the boat like a fountain, and made the whole crowd sit up straight in no time. When he spread more than pint of water over one of those dresses, he would give a pleasant little laugh, and say:

"I beg your pardon, I'm sure;" and offer them his handkerchief to wipe it off with.

"Oh, it's of no consequence," the poor girls would murmur in reply, and covertly draw rugs and coats over themselves, and try and protect themselves with their lace parasols.

At lunch they had a very bad time of it. People wanted them to sit on the grass, and the grass was dusty; and the tree-trunks, against which they were invited to lean, did not appear to have been brushed for weeks; so they spread their handkerchiefs on the ground and sat on those, bolt upright. Somebody, in walking about with a plate of beef-steak pie, tripped up over a root, and sent the pie flying. None of it went over them, fortunately, but the accident suggested a fresh danger to them, and agitated them; and, whenever anybody moved about, after that, with anything in his hand that could fall and make a mess, they watched that person with growing anxiety until he sat down again.

"Now then, you girls," said our friend Bow to them, cheerily, after it was all over, "come along, you've got to wash up!"

They didn't understand him at first. When they grasped the idea, they said they feared they did not know how to wash up.

"Oh, I'll soon show you," he cried; "it's rare fun! You lie down on your - I mean you lean over the bank, you know, and sloush the things about in the water."

The elder sister said that she was afraid that they hadn't got on dresses suited to the work.

"Oh, they'll be all right," said he light-heartedly; "tuck `em up."

And he made them do it, too. He told them that that sort of thing was half the fun of a picnic. They said it was very interesting.

Now I come to think it over, was that young man as dense-headed as we thought? or was he - no, impossible! there was such a simple, child-like expression about him!

Harris wanted to get out at Hampton Church, to go and see Mrs. Thomas's tomb.

"Who is Mrs. Thomas?" I asked.

"How should I know?" replied Harris. "She's a lady that's got a funny tomb, and I want to see it."

I objected. I don't know whether it is that I am built wrong, but I never did seem to hanker after tombstones myself. I know that the proper thing to do, when you get to a village or town, is to rush off to the churchyard, and enjoy the graves; but it is a recreation that I always deny myself. I take no interest in creeping round dim and chilly churches behind wheezy old men, and reading epitaphs. Not even the sight of a bit of cracked brass let into a stone affords me what I call real happiness.

I shock respectable sextons by the imperturbability I am able to assume before exciting inscriptions, and by my lack of enthusiasm for the local family history, while my ill-concealed anxiety to get outside wounds their feelings.

We stopped under the willows by Kempton Park, and lunched. It is a pretty little spot there: a pleasant grass plateau, running along by the water's edge, and overhung by willows. We had just commenced the third course - the bread and jam - when a gentleman in shirt-sleeves and a short pipe came along, and wanted to know if we knew that we were trespassing. We said we hadn't given the matter sufficient consideration as yet to enable us to arrive at a definite conclusion on that point, but that, if he assured us on his word as a gentleman that we *were* trespassing, we would, without further hesitation, believe it.

He gave us the required assurance, and we thanked him, but he still hung about, and seemed to be dissatisfied, so we asked him if there was anything further that we could do for him; and Harris, who is of a chummy disposition, offered him a bit of bread and jam.

I fancy he must have belonged to some society sworn to abstain from bread and jam; for he declined it quite gruffly, as if he were vexed at being tempted with it, and he added that it was his duty to turn us off.

Of course, we never saw him anymore, and, of course, all he really wanted was a shilling. There are a certain number of riverside roughs who make quite an income, during the summer, by slouching about the banks and blackmailing weak-minded noodles in this way. They represent themselves as sent by the proprietor. The proper course to pursue is to offer your name and address, and leave the owner, if he really has anything to do with the matter, to summon you, and prove what damage you have done to his land by sitting down on a bit of it. But the majority of people are so intensely lazy and timid, that they prefer to encourage the imposition by giving in to it rather than put an end to it by the exertion of a little firmness.

L.... in the evening we attended a party. Harris sang to his heart's. We were a fashionable and highly cultured party. We had on our best clothes, and we talked pretty, and were very happy - all except two young fellows, students, just returned from Germany, commonplace young men, who seemed restless and uncomfortable, as if they found the proceedings slow. The truth was, we were too clever for them. Our brilliant but polished conversation, and our high-class tastes, were beyond them. They were out of place, among us. They never ought to have been there at all. Everybody agreed upon that, later on.

We played short musical piece from the old German masters. We discussed philosophy and ethics. We flirted with graceful dignity. We were even humorous - in a high-class way.

Somebody recited a French poem after supper, and we said it was beautiful; and then a lady sang a sentimental ballad in Spanish, and it made one or two of us weep - it was so pathetic.

That was the end of that party. I never saw a party break up so quietly, and with so little fuss. We never said good-night even to one another. We came downstairs one at a time, walking softly, and keeping the shady side. We asked the servant for our hats and coats in whispers, and opened the door for ourselves, and slipped out, and got round the corner quickly, avoiding each other as much as possible.

I have never taken much interest in German songs since then.

We reached Sunbury Lock at half-past three. The river is sweetly pretty just there before you come to the gates, and the backwater is charming; but don't attempt to row up it.

There is an iron "scold's bridle" in Walton Church. They used these things in ancient days for curbing women's tongues. They have given up the attempt now. I suppose iron was getting scarce, and nothing else would be strong enough.

There are also tombs of note in the church, and I was afraid I should never get Harris past them; but he didn't seem to think of them, and we went on. Above the bridge the river winds tremendously. This makes it look picturesque; but it irritates you from a towing or sculling point of view, and causes argument between the man who is pulling and the man who is steering.

You pass Oatlands Park on the right bank here. It is a famous old place. Henry VIII. stole it from some one or the other, I forget whom now, and lived in it. There is a grotto in the park which you can see for a fee, and which is supposed to be very wonderful; but I cannot see much in it myself. The late Duchess of York, who lived at Oatlands, was very fond of dogs, and kept an immense number. She had a special graveyard made, in which to bury them when they died, and there they lie, about fifty of them, with a tombstone over each, and an epitaph inscribed thereon.

Well, I dare say they deserve it quite as much as the average Christian does.

At "Corway Stakes" - the first bend above Walton Bridge - was fought a battle between Cæsar and Cassivelaunus. Cassivelaunus had prepared the river for Cæsar, by planting it full of stakes (and had, no doubt, put up a notice-board). But Cæsar crossed in spite of this. You couldn't choke Cæsar off that river. He is the sort of man we want round the backwaters now.

At Weybridge, the Wey (a pretty little stream, navigable for small boats up to Guildford, and one which I have always been making up my mind to explore, and never have), the Bourne, and the Basingstoke Canal all enter the Thames together. The lock is just opposite the town, and the first thing that we saw, when we came in view of it, was George's blazer on one of the lock gates, closer inspection showing that George was inside it.

Montmorency set up a furious barking, I shrieked, Harris roared; George waved his hat, and yelled back. The lock-keeper rushed out with a drag, under the impression that somebody had fallen into the lock, and appeared annoyed at finding that no one had.

George had rather a curious oilskin-covered parcel in his hand. It was round and flat at one end, with a long straight handle sticking out of it.

"What's that?" said Harris - "a frying-pan?"

"No," said George, with a strange, wild look glittering in his eyes; "they are all the rage this season; everybody has got them up the river. It's a banjo."

"I never knew you played the banjo!" cried Harris and I, in one breath.

"Not exactly," replied George: "but it's very easy, they tell me; and I've got the instruction book!"

❐

Chapter 5

First Night Under Canvas

We made George work, now we had got him. He did not want to work, of course; that goes without saying. He had had a hard time in the City, so he explained. Harris, who is callous in his nature, and not prone to pity, said:

"Ah! and now you are going to have a hard time on the river for a change; change is good for everyone. Out you get!"

He could not in conscience - not even George's conscience - object, though he did suggest that, perhaps, it would be better for him to stop in the boat, and get tea ready, while Harris and I towed, because getting tea was such a worrying work, and Harris and I looked tired. The only reply we made to this, however, was to pass him over the tow-line, and he took it, and stepped out.

There is something very strange and unaccountable about a tow-line. You roll it up with as much patience and care as you would take to fold up a new pair of trousers, and five minutes afterwards, when you pick it up, it is one ghastly, soul-revolting tangle.

I do not wish to be insulting, but I firmly believe that if you took an average tow-line, and stretched it out straight across the middle of a field, and then turned your back on it for thirty seconds, that, when you looked round again, you would find that it had got itself altogether in a heap in the middle of the field, and had twisted itself up, and tied itself into knots, and lost its two ends, and become all loops; and it would take you a good half-hour, sitting down there on the grass and swearing all the while, to disentangle it again.

That is my opinion of tow-lines in general. Of course, there may be honourable exceptions; I do not say that there are not. There may be tow-lines that are a credit to their profession - conscientious, respectable tow-lines - tow-lines that do not imagine they are crochet-work, and try to knit themselves up into antimacassars the instant they are left to themselves. I say there *may* be such tow-lines; I sincerely hope there are. But I have not met with them.

This tow-line I had taken in myself just before we had got to the lock. I would not let Harris touch it, because he is careless. I had looped it round slowly and cautiously, and tied it up in the middle, and folded it in two, and laid it down gently at the bottom of the boat. Harris had lifted it up scientifically, and had put it into George's hand. George had taken it firmly, and held it away from him, and had begun to unravel it as if he were taking the swaddling clothes off a new-born infant; and, before he had unwound a dozen yards, the thing was more like a badly-made door-mat than anything else.

It is always the same, and the same sort of thing always goes on in connection with it. The man on the bank, who is trying to disentangle it, thinks all the fault lies with the man who rolled it up; and when a man up the river thinks a thing, he says it.

"What have you been trying to do with it, make a fishing-net of it? You've made a nice mess you have; why couldn't you wind it up properly, you silly

The first man gives a yell and goes mad.

dummy?" he grunts from time to time as he struggles wildly with it, and lays it out flat on the tow-path, and runs round and round it, trying to find the end.

On the other hand, the man who wound it up thinks the whole cause of the muddle rests with the man who is trying to unwind it.

"It was all right when you took it!" he exclaims indignantly. "Why don't you think what you are doing? You go about things in such a slap-dash style. You'd get a scaffolding pole entangled you would!"

And they feel so angry with one another that they would like to hang each other with the thing. Ten minutes go by, and the first man gives a yell and goes mad, and dances on the rope, and tries to pull it straight by seizing hold of the first piece that comes to his hand and hauling at it. Of course, this only gets it into a tighter tangle than ever. Then the second man climbs out of the boat and comes to help him, and they get in each other's way, and hinder one another. They both get hold of the same bit of line, and pull at it in opposite directions, and wonder where it is caught. In the end, they do get it clear, and then turn round and find that the boat has drifted off, and is making straight for the weir.

Harris and I began to think that Bell Weir lock must have been done away with after the same manner. George had towed us up to Staines, and we had taken the boat from there, and it seemed that we were dragging fifty tons after us, and were walking forty miles. It was half-past seven when we were through, and we all got in, and sculled up close to the left bank, looking out for a spot to haul up in.

We had originally intended to go on to Magna Charta Island, a sweetly pretty part of the river, where it winds through a soft, green valley, and to camp in one of the many picturesque inlets to be found round that tiny shore. But, somehow, we did not feel that we yearned for the picturesque nearly so much now as we had earlier in the day. A bit of water between a coal-barge and a gas-works would have quite satisfied us for that night. We did not want scenery. We wanted to have our supper and go to bed. However, we did pull up to the point - "Picnic Point," it is called - and dropped into a very pleasant nook under a great elm-tree, to the spreading roots of which we fastened the boat.

Then we thought we were going to have supper (we had dispensed with tea, so as to save time), but George said no; that we had better get the canvas up first, before it got quite dark, and while we could see what we were doing. Then, he said, all our work would be done, and we could sit down to eat with an easy mind.

That canvas wanted more putting up than I think any of us had bargained for. It looked so simple in the abstract. You took five iron arches, like gigantic croquet hoops, and fitted them up over the boat, and then stretched the canvas over them, and fastened it down: it would take quite ten minutes, we thought.

That was an under-estimate.

We took up the hoops, and began to drop them into the sockets placed for them. You would not imagine this to be dangerous work; but, looking back now, the wonder to me is that any of us are alive to tell the tale. They were not hoops, they were demons. First they would not fit into their sockets at all, and we had to jump on them, and kick them, and hammer at them with the boat-hook; and, when they were in, it turned out that they were the wrong hoops for those particular sockets, and they had to come out again.

But they would not come out, until two of us had gone and struggled with them for five minutes, when they would jump up suddenly, and try and throw us into the water and drown us. They had hinges in the middle, and, when we were not looking, they nipped us with these hinges in delicate parts of the body; and, while we were wrestling with one side of the hoop, and endeavouring to persuade it to do its duty, the other side would come behind us in a cowardly manner, and hit us over the head.

We got them fixed at last, and then all that was to be done was to arrange the covering over them. George unrolled it, and fastened one end over the nose of the boat. Harris stood in the middle to take it from George and roll it on to me, and I kept by the stern to receive it. It was a long time coming down to me. George did his part all right, but it was new work to Harris, and he bungled it.

How he managed it I do not know, he could not explain himself; but by some mysterious process or other he succeeded, after ten minutes of superhuman effort, in getting himself completely rolled up in it. He was so firmly wrapped round and tucked in and folded over, that he could not get out. He, of course, made frantic struggles for freedom - the birthright of every Englishman, - and, in doing so (I learned this afterwards), knocked over George; and then George, swearing at Harris, began to struggle too, and got *himself* entangled and rolled up.

I knew nothing about all this at the time. I did not understand the business at all myself. I had been told to stand where I was, and wait till the canvas came to me, and Montmorency and I stood there and waited, both as good as gold. We could see the canvas being violently jerked and tossed about, pretty considerably; but we supposed this was part of the method, and did not interfere.

We also heard much smothered language coming from underneath it, and we guessed that they were finding the job rather troublesome, and concluded that we would wait until things had got a little simpler before we joined in.

We waited some time, but matters seemed to get only more and more involved, until, at last, George's head came wriggling out over the side of the boat, and spoke up.

It said: "Give us a hand here, can't you, you cuckoo; standing there like a stuffed mummy, when you see we are both being suffocated, you dummy!"

I never could withstand an appeal for help, so I went and undid them; not before it was time, either, for Harris was nearly black in the face.

It took us half an hour's hard labour, after that, before it was properly up, and then we cleared the decks, and got out supper. We put the kettle on to boil, up in the nose of the boat, and went down to the stern and pretended to take no notice of it, but set to work to get the other things out.

That is the only way to get a kettle to boil up the river. If it sees that you are waiting for it and are anxious, it will never even sing. You have to go away and begin your meal, as if you were not going to have any tea at all. You must not even look round at it. Then you will soon hear it sputtering away, mad to be made into tea.

It is a good plan, too, if you are in a great hurry, to talk very loudly to each other about how you don't need any tea, and are not going to have any. You get near the kettle, so that it can overhear you, and then you shout out, "I don't want any tea; do you, George?" to which George shouts back, "Oh, no, I don't like tea; we'll have lemonade instead - tea's so indigestible." Upon which the kettle boils over, and puts the stove out.

We adopted this harmless bit of trickery, and the result was that, by the time everything else was ready, the tea was waiting. Then we lit the lantern, and squatted down to supper.

We wanted that supper.

For five-and-thirty minutes not a sound was heard throughout the length and breadth of that boat, save the clank of cutlery and crockery, and the steady grinding of four sets of molars. At the end of five-and-thirty minutes, Harris said, "Ah!" and took his left leg out from under him and put his right one there instead.

Five minutes afterwards, George said, "Ah!" too, and threw his plate out on the bank; and, three minutes later than that, Montmorency gave the first sign of contentment he had exhibited since we had started, and rolled over on his side, and spread his legs out; and then I said, "Ah!" and bent my head back, and bumped it against one of the hoops, but I did not mind it. I did not even swear.

How good one feels when one is full - how satisfied with ourselves and with the world! People who have tried it, tell me that a clear conscience makes you very happy and contented; but a full stomach does the business quite as well, and is cheaper, and more easily obtained. One feels so forgiving and generous after a substantial and well-digested meal - so noble-minded, so kindly-hearted.

It is very strange, this domination of our intellect by our digestive organs. We cannot work, we cannot think, unless our stomach wills so.

Before our supper, Harris and George and I were quarrelsome and snappy and ill-tempered; after our supper, we sat and beamed on one another, and we beamed upon the dog, too. We loved each other, we loved everybody. Harris, in moving about, trod on George's corn. Had this happened before supper, George would have expressed wishes and desires concerning Harris's fate in this world and the next that would have made a thoughtful man shudder.

As it was, he said: "Steady, old man; `ware wheat."

And Harris, instead of merely observing, in his most unpleasant tones, that a fellow could hardly help treading on some bit of George's foot, if he had to move about at all within ten yards of where George was sitting, suggesting that George never ought to come into an ordinary sized boat with feet that length, and advising him to hang them over the side, as he would have done before supper, now said: "Oh, I'm so sorry, old chap; I hope I haven't hurt you."

And George said: "Not at all;" that it was his fault; and Harris said no, it was his.

It was quite pretty to hear them.

We lit our pipes, and sat, looking out on the quiet night, and talked.

We turned in at ten that night, and I thought I should sleep well, being tired; but I didn't. As a rule, I undress and put my head on the pillow, and then somebody bangs at the door, and says it is half-past eight: but, to-night, everything seemed against me; the novelty of it all, the hardness of the boat, the cramped position (I was lying with my feet under one seat, and my head on another), the sound of the lapping water round the boat, and the wind among the branches, kept me restless and disturbed.

I did get to sleep for a few hours, and then some part of the boat which seemed to have grown up in the night - for it certainly was not there when we started, and it had disappeared by the morning - kept digging into my spine. I slept through it for a while, dreaming that I had swallowed a sovereign, and that they were cutting a hole in my back with a gimlet, so as to try and get it out. I thought it very unkind of them, and I told them I would owe them the money, and they should have it at the end of the month. But they would not hear of that, and said it would be much better if they had it then, because otherwise the interest would accumulate so. I got quite cross with them after a bit, and told them what I thought of them, and then they gave the gimlet such an excruciating wrench that I woke up.

The boat seemed stuffy, and my head ached; so I thought I would step out into the cool night-air. I slipped on what clothes I could find about - some of my own, and some of George's and Harris's - and crept under the canvas on to the bank.

It was a glorious night. The moon had sunk, and left the quiet earth alone with the stars. It seemed as if, in the silence and the hush, while we her children slept, they were talking with her, their sister - conversing of mighty mysteries in voices too vast and deep for childish human ears to catch the sound.

❐

Chapter 6

An Angel Comes By

I woke at six the next morning; and found George awake too. We both turned round, and tried to go to sleep again, but we could not. Had there been any particular reason why we should not have gone to sleep again, but have got up and dressed then and there, we should have dropped off while we were looking at our watches, and have slept till ten. As there was no earthly necessity for our getting up under another two hours at the very least, and our getting up at that time was an utter absurdity, it was only in keeping with the natural cussedness of things in general that we should both feel that lying down for five minutes more would be death to us.

We had been sitting huddled up in our rugs while George had been telling me his true story, and on his finishing it I set to work to wake up Harris with a scull. The third prod did it: and he turned over on the other side, and said he would be down in a minute, and that he would have his lace-up boots. We soon let him know where he was, however, by the aid of the hitcher, and he sat up suddenly, sending Montmorency, who had been sleeping the sleep of the just right on the middle of his chest, sprawling across the boat.

Then we pulled up the canvas, and all four of us poked our heads out over the off-side, and looked down at the water and shivered. The idea, overnight, had been that we should get up early in the morning, fling off our rugs and shawls, and, throwing back the canvas, spring into the river with a joyous shout, and revel in a long delicious swim. Somehow, now the morning had come, the notion seemed less tempting. The water looked damp and chilly: the wind felt cold.

"Well, who's going to be first in?" said Harris at last.

There was no rush for precedence. George settled the matter so far as he was concerned by retiring into the boat and pulling on his socks. Montmorency gave vent to an involuntary howl, as if merely thinking of the thing had given him the horrors; and Harris said it would be so difficult to get into the boat again, and went back and sorted out his trousers.

I did not altogether like to give in, though I did not relish the plunge. There might be snags about, or weeds, I thought. I meant to compromise matters by going down to the edge and just throwing the water over myself; so I took a towel and crept out on the bank and wormed my way along on to the branch of a tree that dipped down into the water.

It was bitterly cold. The wind cut like a knife. I thought I would not throw the water over myself after all. I would go back into the boat and dress; and I turned to do so; and, as I turned, the silly branch gave way, and I and the towel went in together with a tremendous splash, and I was out mid-stream with a gallon of Thames water inside me before I knew what had happened.

"By Jove! old J.'s gone in," I heard Harris say, as I came blowing to the surface. "I didn't think he'd have the pluck to do it. Did you?"

"Lovely," I spluttered back.
"You are duffers not to come in."

"Is it all right?" sung out George.

"Lovely," I spluttered back. "You are duffers not to come in. I wouldn't have missed this for worlds. Why won't you try it? It only wants a little determination."

But I could not persuade them.

Rather an amusing thing happened while dressing that morning. I was very cold when I got back into the boat, and, in my hurry to get my shirt on, I accidentally jerked it into the water. It made me awfully wild, especially as George burst out laughing. I could not see anything to laugh at, and I told George so, and he only laughed the more. I never saw a man laugh so much. I quite lost my temper with him at last, and I pointed out to him what a drivelling maniac of an imbecile idiot he was; but he only roared the louder. And then, just as I was landing the shirt, I noticed that it was not my shirt at all, but George's, which I had mistaken for mine; whereupon the humour of the thing struck me for the first time, and *I* began to laugh. And the more I looked from George's wet shirt to George, roaring with laughter, the more I was amused, and I laughed so much that I had to let the shirt fall back into the water again.

"Ar'n't you - you - going to get it out?" said George, between his shrieks.

I could not answer him at all for a while, I was laughing so, but, at last, between my peals I managed to jerk out:

"It isn't my shirt - it's *yours!*"

I never saw a man's face change from lively to severe so suddenly in all my life before.

Harris proposed that we should have scrambled eggs for breakfast. He said he would cook them. It seemed, from his account, that he was very good at doing scrambled eggs. He often did them at picnics and when out on yachts. He was quite famous for them. People who had once tasted his scrambled eggs, so we gathered from his conversation, never cared for any other food afterwards, but pined away and died when they could not get them.

It made our mouths water to hear him talk about the things, and we handed him out the stove and the frying-pan and all the eggs that had not smashed and gone over everything in the hamper, and begged him to begin.

He had some trouble in breaking the eggs - or rather not so much trouble in breaking them exactly as in getting them into the frying-pan when broken, and keeping them off his trousers, and preventing them from running up his sleeve; but he fixed some half-a-dozen into the pan at last, and then squatted down by the side of the stove and chivied them about with a fork.

It seemed harassing work, so far as George and I could judge. Whenever he went near the pan he burned himself, and then he would drop everything and dance round the stove, flicking his fingers about and cursing the things. Indeed, every time George and I looked round at him he was sure to be performing this feat. We thought at first that it was a necessary part of the culinary arrangements.

We did not know what scrambled eggs were, and we fancied that it must be some Red Indian or Sandwich Islands sort of dish that required dances and incantations for its proper cooking. Montmorency went and put his nose over it once, and the fat spluttered up and scalded him, and then *he* began dancing and cursing. Altogether it was one of the most interesting and exciting operations I have ever witnessed. George and I were both quite sorry when it was over.

The result was not altogether the success that Harris had anticipated. There seemed so little to show for the business. Six eggs had gone into the frying-pan, and all that came out was a teaspoonful of burnt and unappetizing looking mess.

Harris said it was the fault of the frying-pan, and thought it would have gone better if we had had a fish-kettle and a gas-stove; and we decided not to attempt the dish again until we had those aids to housekeeping by us.

Slowly the heavy, bright-decked barges leave the shore of Runningmede. Slowly against the swift current they work their ponderous way, till, with a low grumble, they grate against the bank of the little island that from this day will bear the name of Magna Charta Island. And King John has stepped upon the shore, and we wait in breathless silence till a great shout cleaves the air, and the great cornerstone in England's temple of liberty has, now we know, been firmly laid.

I was sitting on the bank, conjuring up this scene to myself, when George remarked that when I was quite rested, perhaps I would not mind helping to wash up; and, thus recalled from the days of the glorious past to the prosaic present, with all its misery and sin, I slid down into the boat and cleaned out the frying-pan with a stick of wood and a tuft of grass, polishing it up finally with George's wet shirt.

We went over to Magna Charta Island, and had a look at the stone which stands in the cottage there and on which the great Charter is said to have been signed; though, as to whether it really was signed there, or, as some say, on the other bank at "Runningmede," I decline to commit myself. As far as my own personal opinion goes, however, I am inclined to give weight to the popular island theory. Certainly, had I been one of the Barons, at the time, I should have strongly urged upon my comrades the advisability of our getting such a slippery customer as King John on to the island, where there was less chance of surprises and tricks.

There are the ruins of an old priory in the grounds of Ankerwyke House, which is close to Picnic Point, and it was round about the grounds of this old priory that Henry VIII. is said to have waited for and met Anne Boleyn. He also used to meet her at Hever Castle in Kent, and also somewhere near St. Albans. It must have been difficult for the people of England in those days to have found a spot where these thoughtless young folk were *not* spooning.

Have you ever been in a house where there are a couple courting? It is most trying. You think you will go and sit in the drawing-room, and you march off there. As you open the door, you hear a noise as if somebody had suddenly recollected something, and, when you get in, Emily is over by the window, full of interest in the opposite side of the road, and your friend, John Edward, is at the other end of the room with his whole soul held in thrall by photographs of other people's relatives.

"Oh!" you say, pausing at the door, "I didn't know anybody was here."

"Oh! didn't you?" says Emily, coldly, in a tone which implies that she does not believe you.

You hang about for a bit, then you say, "It's very dark. Why don't you light the gas?"

John Edward says, "Oh!" he hadn't noticed it; and Emily says that papa does not like the gas lit in the afternoon.

You tell them one or two items of news, and give them your views and opinions on the Irish question; but this does not appear to interest them. All they remark on any subject is, "Oh!" "Is it?" "Did he?" "Yes," and "You don't say so!" And, after ten minutes of such style of conversation, you edge up to the door, and slip out, and are surprised to find that the door immediately closes behind you, and shuts itself, without your having touched it.

Half an hour later, you think you will try a pipe in the conservatory. The only chair in the place is occupied by Emily; and John Edward, if the language of clothes can be relied upon, has evidently been sitting on the floor. They do not speak, but they give you a look that says all that can be said in a civilised community; and you back out promptly and shut the door behind you.

You are afraid to poke your nose into any room in the house now; so, after walking up and down the stairs for a while, you go and sit in your own bedroom. This becomes uninteresting, however, after a time, and so you put on your hat and stroll out into the garden. You walk down the path, and as you pass the summer-house you glance in, and there are those two young idiots, huddled up into one corner of it; and they see you, and are evidently under the idea that, for some wicked purpose of your own, you are following them about.

"Why don't they have a special room for this sort of thing, and make people keep to it?" you mutter; and you rush back to the hall and get your umbrella and go out.

It must have been much like this when that foolish boy Henry VIII was courting his little Anne. People in Buckinghamshire would have come upon them unexpectedly when they were mooning round Windsor and Wraysbury, and have exclaimed, "Oh! you here!" and Henry would have blushed and said, "Yes; he'd just come over to see a man;" and Anne would have said, "Oh, I'm so glad to see you! Isn't it funny? I've just met Mr. Henry VIII. in the lane, and he's going the same way I am."

Then those people would have gone away and said to themselves: "Oh! we'd better get out of here while this billing and cooing is on. We'll go down to Kent."

And they would go to Kent, and the first thing they would see in Kent, when they got there, would be Henry and Anne fooling round Hever Castle.

"Oh, drat this!" they would have said. "Here, let's go away. I can't stand any more of it. Let's go to St. Albans - nice quiet place, St. Albans."

And when they reached St. Albans, there would be that wretched couple, kissing under the Abbey walls. Then these folks would go and be pirates until the marriage was over.

"If I am guilty," said the Earl, "may this bread choke me when I eat it!"

Then he put the bread into his mouth and swallowed it, and it choked him, and he died.

After you have passed Old Windsor, the river is somewhat uninteresting, and does not become itself again until you are nearing Boveney. George and I towed up past the Home Park, which stretches along the right bank from Albert to Victoria Bridge; and as we were passing Datchet, George asked me if I remembered our first trip up the river, and when we landed at Datchet at ten o'clock at night, and wanted to go to bed.

I answered that I did remember it. It will be some time before I forget it.

It was the Saturday before the August Bank Holiday. We were tired and hungry, we same three, and when we got to Datchet we took out the hamper, the two bags, and the rugs and coats, and such like things, and started off to look for diggings. We passed a very pretty little hotel, with clematis and creeper over the porch; but there was no honeysuckle about it, and, for some reason or other, I had got my mind fixed on honeysuckle, and I said:

"Oh, don't let's go in there! Let's go on a bit further, and see if there isn't one with honeysuckle over it."

So we went on till we came to another hotel. That was a very nice hotel, too, and it had honey-suckle on it, round at the side; but Harris did not like the look of a man who was leaning against the front door. He said he didn't look a nice man at all, and he wore ugly boots: so we went on further. We went a goodish way without coming across any more hotels, and then we met a man, and asked him to direct us to a few.

He said:

"Why, you are coming away from them. You must turn right round and go back, and then you will come to the Stag."

We said:

"Oh, we had been there, and didn't like it - no honeysuckle over it."

The landlord came up and said,
"Good evening, gentlemen."

"Well, then," he said, "there's the Manor House, just opposite. Have you tried that?"

Harris replied that we did not want to go there - didn't like the looks of a man who was stopping there - Harris did not like the colour of his hair, didn't like his boots, either.

"Well, I don't know what you'll do, I'm sure," said our informant; "because they are the only two inns in the place."

"No other inns!" exclaimed Harris.

"None," replied the man.

"What on earth are we to do?" cried Harris.

Then George spoke up. He said Harris and I could get an hotel built for us, if we liked, and have some people made to put in. For his part, he was going back to the Stag.

The greatest minds never realise their ideals in any matter; and Harris and I sighed over the hollowness of all earthly desires, and followed George.

We took our traps into the Stag, and laid them down in the hall.

The landlord came up and said:

"Good evening, gentlemen."

"Oh, good evening," said George; "we want three beds, please."

"Very sorry, sir," said the landlord; "but I'm afraid we can't manage it."

"Oh, well, never mind," said George, "two will do. Two of us can sleep in one bed, can't we?" he continued, turning to Harris and me.

Harris said, "Oh, yes;" he thought George and I could sleep in one bed very easily.

"Very sorry, sir," again repeated the landlord: "but we really haven't got a bed vacant in the whole house.

In fact, we are putting two, and even three gentlemen in one bed, as it is."

This staggered us for a bit.

But Harris, who is an old traveller, rose to the occasion, and, laughing cheerily, said:

"Oh, well, we can't help it. We must rough it. You must give us a shake-down in the billiard-room."

"Very sorry, sir. Three gentlemen sleeping on the billiard-table already, and two in the coffee-room. Can't possibly take you in tonight."

We picked up our things, and went over to the Manor House. It was a pretty little place. I said I thought I should like it better than the other house; and Harris said, "Oh, yes," it would be all right, and we needn't look at the man with the red hair; besides, the poor fellow couldn't help having red hair.

Harris spoke quite kindly and sensibly about it.

Then we went back into the high road, and Harris sat down on the hamper and said he would go no further. He said it seemed a quiet spot, and he would like to die there. He requested George and me to kiss his mother for him, and to tell all his relations that he forgave them and died happy.

At that moment an angel came by in the disguise of a small boy (and I cannot think of any more effective disguise an angel could have assumed), with a can of beer in one hand, and in the other something at the end of a string, which he let down on to every flat stone he came across, and then pulled up again, this producing a peculiarly unattractive sound, suggestive of suffering.

We asked this heavenly messenger (as we discovered him afterwards to be) if he knew of any lonely house, whose occupants were few and feeble (old ladies or paralysed gentlemen preferred), who could be easily frightened into giving up their beds for the night to three desperate men; or, if not this, could he recommend us to an empty pigstye, or a disused limekiln, or anything of that sort. He did not know of any such place - at least, not one handy; but he said that, if we liked to come with him, his mother had a room to spare, and could put us up for the night.

We fell upon his neck there in the moonlight and blessed him, and it would have made a very beautiful picture if the boy himself had not been so over-powered by our emotion as to be unable to sustain himself under it, and sunk to the ground, letting us all down on top of him. Harris was so overcome with joy that he fainted, and had to seize the boy's beer-can and half empty it before he could recover consciousness, and then he started off at a run, and left George and me to bring on the luggage.

To return to our present trip: nothing exciting happened, and we tugged steadily on to a little below Monkey Island, where we drew up and lunched. We tackled the cold beef for lunch, and then we found that we had forgotten to bring any mustard. I don't think I ever in my life, before or since, felt I wanted mustard as badly as I felt I wanted it then. I don't care for mustard as a rule, and it is very seldom that I take it at all, but I would have given worlds for it then.

I don't know how many worlds there may be in the universe, but anyone who had brought me a spoonful of mustard at that precise moment could have had them all. I grow reckless like that when I want a thing and can't get it.

Harris said he would have given worlds for mustard too. It would have been a good thing for anybody who had come up to that spot with a can of mustard, then:

he would have been set up in worlds for the rest of his life.

But there! I daresay both Harris and I would have tried to back out of the bargain after we had got the mustard. One makes these extravagant offers in moments of excitement, but, of course, when one comes to think of it, one sees how absurdly out of proportion they are with the value of the required article. I heard a man, going up a mountain in Switzerland, once say he would give worlds for a glass of beer, and, when he came to a little shanty where they kept it, he kicked up a most fearful row because they charged him five francs for a bottle of Bass. He said it was a scandalous imposition, and he wrote to *The Times* about it.

It cast a gloom over the boat, there being no mustard. We ate our beef in silence. Existence seemed hollow and uninteresting. We thought of the happy days of childhood, and sighed. We brightened up a bit, however, over the apple-tart, and, when George drew out a tin of pine-apple from the bottom of the hamper, and rolled it into the middle of the boat, we felt that life was worth living after all.

We are very fond of pine-apple, all three of us. We looked at the picture on the tin; we thought of the juice. We smiled at one another, and Harris got a spoon ready.

Then we looked for the knife to open the tin with. We turned out everything in the hamper. We turned out the bags. We pulled up the boards at the bottom of the boat. We took everything out on to the bank and shook it. There was no tin-opener to be found.

Then Harris tried to open the tin with a pocket-knife, and broke the knife and cut himself badly; and George tried a pair of scissors, and the scissors flew up, and nearly put his eye out. While they were dressing their wounds, I tried to make a hole in the thing with the spiky end of the hitcher, and the hitcher slipped and jerked me out between the boat and the bank into two feet of muddy water, and the tin rolled over, uninjured, and broke a teacup.

Then we all got mad. We took that tin out on the bank, and Harris went up into a field and got a big sharp stone, and I went back into the boat and brought out the mast, and George held the tin and Harris held the sharp end of his stone against the top of it, and I took the mast and poised it high up in the air, and gathered up all my strength and brought it down.

It was George's straw hat that saved his life that day. He keeps that hat now (what is left of it), and, of a winter's evening, when the pipes are lit and the boys are telling stretchers about the dangers they have passed through, George brings it down and shows it round, and the stirring tale is told anew, with fresh exaggerations every time.

Harris got off with merely a flesh wound.

After that, I took the tin off myself, and hammered at it with the mast till I was worn out and sick at heart, whereupon Harris took it in hand.

We beat it out flat; we beat it back square; we battered it into every form known to geometry - but we could not make a hole in it. Then George went at it, and knocked it into a shape, so strange, so weird, so unearthly in its wild hideousness, that he got frightened and threw away the mast. Then we all three sat round it on the grass and looked at it.

❐

Chapter 7

Fight between Montmorency and Tea-kettle

Marlow is one of the pleasantest river centres I know of. It is a bustling, lively little town; not very picturesque on the whole, it is true, but there are many quaint nooks and corners to be found in it, nevertheless - standing arches in the shattered bridge of Time, over which our fancy travels back to the days when Marlow Manor owned Saxon Algar for its lord, ere conquering William seized it to give to Queen Matilda, ere it passed to the Earls of Warwick or to worldly-wise Lord Paget, the councillor of four successive sovereigns.

I remember being in the lobby of the Haymarket Stores one day, and all round about me were dogs, waiting for the return of their owners, who were shopping inside. There were a mastiff, and one or two collies, and a St. Bernard, a few retrievers and Newfoundlands, a boar-hound, a French poodle, with plenty of hair round its head, but mangy about the middle; a bull-dog, a few Lowther Arcade sort of animals, about the size of rats, and a couple of Yorkshire tykes.

There they sat, patient, good, and thoughtful. A solemn peacefulness seemed to reign in that lobby. An air of calmness and resignation - of gentle sadness pervaded the room.

Then a sweet young lady entered, leading a meek-looking little fox-terrier, and left him, chained up there, between the bull-dog and the poodle. He sat and looked about him for a minute. Then he cast up his eyes to the ceiling, and seemed, judging from his expression, to be thinking of his mother. Then he yawned. Then he looked round at the other dogs, all silent, grave, and dignified.

He looked at the bull-dog, sleeping dreamlessly on his right. He looked at the poodle, erect and haughty, on his left. Then, without a word of warning, without the shadow of a provocation, he bit that poodle's near fore-leg, and a yelp of agony rang through the quiet shades of that lobby.

The result of his first experiment seemed highly satisfactory to him, and he determined to go on and make things lively all round. He sprang over the poodle and vigorously attacked a collie, and the collie woke up, and immediately commenced a fierce and noisy contest with the poodle. Then Foxey came back to his own place, and caught the bull-dog by the ear, and tried to throw him away; and the bull-dog, a curiously impartial animal, went for everything he could reach, including the hall-porter, which gave that dear little terrier the opportunity to enjoy an uninterrupted fight of his own with an equally willing Yorkshire tyke.

Anyone who knows canine nature need hardly, be told that, by this time, all the other dogs in the place were fighting as if their hearths and homes depended on the fray. The big dogs fought each other indiscriminately; and the little dogs fought among themselves, and filled up their spare time by biting the legs of the big dogs.

I don't blame Montmorency for his tendency to row with cats.

The whole lobby was a perfect pandemonium, and the din was terrific. A crowd assembled outside in the Haymarket, and asked if it was a vestry meeting; or, if not, who was being murdered, and why? Men came with poles and ropes, and tried to separate the dogs, and the police were sent for.

And in the midst of the riot that sweet young lady returned, and snatched up that sweet little dog of hers (he had laid the tyke up for a month, and had on the expression, now, of a new-born lamb) into her arms, and kissed him, and asked him if he was killed, and what those great nasty brutes of dogs had been doing to him; and he nestled up against her, and gazed up into her face with a look that seemed to say: "Oh, I'm so glad you've come to take me away from this disgraceful scene!"

She said that the people at the Stores had no right to allow great savage things like those other dogs to be put with respectable people's dogs, and that she had a great mind to summon somebody.

Such is the nature of fox-terriers; and, therefore, I do not blame Montmorency for his tendency to row with cats; but he wished he had not given way to it that morning.

Our departure from Marlow I regard as one of our greatest successes. It was dignified and impressive, without being ostentatious. We had insisted at all the shops we had been to that the things should be sent with us then and there. None of your "Yes, sir, I will send them off at once: the boy will be down there before you are, sir!" and then fooling about on the landing-stage, and going back to the shop twice to have a row about them, for us. We waited while the basket was packed, and took the boy with us.

We went to a good many shops, adopting this principle at each one; and the consequence was that, by the time we had finished, we had as fine a collection of boys with baskets following us around as heart could desire; and our final march down the middle of the High Street, to the river, must have been as imposing a spectacle as Marlow had seen for many a long day.

The order of the procession was as follows:-

Montmorency, carrying a stick.

Two disreputable-looking curs, friends of Montmorency's.

George, carrying coats and rugs, and smoking a short pipe.

Harris, trying to walk with easy grace, while carrying a bulged-out Gladstone bag in one hand and a bottle of lime-juice in the other.

Greengrocer's boy and baker's boy, with baskets.

Boots from the hotel, carrying hamper.

Confectioner's boy, with basket.

Grocer's boy, with basket.

Long-haired dog.

Cheesemonger's boy, with basket.

Odd man carrying a bag.

Bosom companion of odd man, with his hands in his pockets, smoking a short clay.

Fruiterer's boy, with basket.

Myself, carrying three hats and a pair of boots, and trying to look as if I didn't know it.

Six small boys, and four stray dogs.

We caught a breeze, after lunch, which took us gently up past Wargrave and Shiplake. Mellowed in the drowsy sunlight of a summer's afternoon, Wargrave, nestling where the river bends, makes a sweet old picture as you pass it, and one that lingers long upon the retina of memory.

The "George and Dragon" at Wargrave boasts a sign, painted on the one side by Leslie, R.A., and on the other by Hodgson of that ilk. Leslie has depicted the fight; Hodgson has imagined the scene, "After the Fight" - George, the work done, enjoying his pint of beer.

Day, the author of *Sandford and Merton,* lived and - more credit to the place still - was killed at Wargrave. In the church is a memorial to Mrs. Sarah Hill, who bequeathed 1 pound annually, to be divided at Easter, between two boys and two girls who "have never been undutiful to their parents; who have never been known to swear or to tell untruths, to steal, or to break windows." Fancy giving up all that for five shillings a year! It is not worth it.

It is rumoured in the town that once, many years ago, a boy appeared who really never had done these things - or at all events, which was all that was required or could be expected, had never been known to do them - and thus won the crown of glory. He was exhibited for three weeks afterwards in the Town Hall, under a glass case.

What has become of the money since no one knows. They say it is always handed over to the nearest wax-works show.

Shiplake is a pretty village, but it cannot be seen from the river, being upon the hill. Tennyson was married in Shiplake Church.

The river up to Sonning winds in and out through many islands, and is very placid, hushed, and lonely. Few folk, except at twilight, a pair or two of rustic lovers, walk along its banks. 'Arry and Lord Fitznoodle have been left behind at Henley, and dismal, dirty Reading is not yet reached. It is a part of the river in which to dream of bygone days, and vanished forms and faces, and things that might have been, but are not, confound them.

We got out at Sonning, and went for a walk round the village. It is the most fairy-like little nook on the whole river. It is more like a stage village than one built of bricks and mortar. Every house is smothered in roses, and now, in early June, they were bursting forth in clouds of dainty splendour. If you stop at Sonning, put up at the "Bull," behind the church. It is a veritable picture of an old country inn, with green, square courtyard in front, where, on seats beneath the trees, the old men group of an evening to drink their ale and gossip over village politics; with low, quaint rooms and latticed windows, and awkward stairs and winding passages.

We roamed about sweet Sonning for an hour or so, and then, it being too late to push on past Reading, we decided to go back to one of the Shiplake islands, and put up there for the night. It was still early when we got settled, and George said that, as we had plenty of time, it would be a splendid opportunity to try a good, slap-up supper. He said he would show us what could be done up the river in the way of cooking, and suggested that, with the vegetables and the remains of the cold beef and general odds and ends, we should make an Irish stew.

It seemed a fascinating idea. George gathered wood and made a fire, and Harris and I started to peel the potatoes. I should never have thought that peeling potatoes was such an undertaking. The job turned out to be the biggest thing of its kind that I had ever been in. We began cheerfully, one might almost say skittishly, but our light-heartedness was gone by the time the first potato was finished. The more we peeled, the more peel there seemed to be left on; by the time we had got all the peel off and all the eyes out, there was no potato left - at least none worth speaking of. George came and had a look at it - it was about the size of a pea-nut. He said, "Oh, that won't do! You're wasting them. You must scrape them."

So we scraped them, and that was harder work than peeling. They are such an extraordinary shape, potatoes - all bumps and warts and hollows. We worked steadily for five-and-twenty minutes, and did four potatoes. Then we struck. We said we should require the rest of the evening for scraping ourselves.

I never saw such a thing as potato-scraping for making a fellow in a mess. It seemed difficult to believe that the potato-scrapings in which Harris and I stood, half smothered, could have come off four potatoes. It shows you what can be done with economy and care.

George said it was absurd to have only four potatoes in an Irish stew, so we washed half-a-dozen or so more, and put them in without peeling. We also put in a cabbage and about half a peck of peas. George stirred it all up, and then he said that there seemed to be a lot of room to spare, so we overhauled both the hampers, and picked out all the odds and ends and the remnants, and added them to the stew. There were half a pork pie and a bit of cold boiled bacon left, and we put them in. Then George found half a tin of potted salmon, and he emptied that into the pot.

We had a discussion as to whether the rat should go in or not.

He said that was the advantage of Irish stew: you got rid of such a lot of things. I fished out a couple of eggs that had got cracked, and put those in. George said they would thicken the gravy.

I forget the other ingredients, but I know nothing was wasted; and I remember that, towards the end, Montmorency, who had evinced great interest in the proceedings throughout, strolled away with an earnest and thoughtful air, reappearing, a few minutes afterwards, with a dead water-rat in his mouth, which he evidently wished to present as his contribution to the dinner; whether in a sarcastic spirit, or with a genuine desire to assist, I cannot say.

We had a discussion as to whether the rat should go in or not. Harris said that he thought it would be all right, mixed up with the other things, and that every little helped; but George stood up for precedent. He said he had never heard of water-rats in Irish stew, and he would rather be on the safe side, and not try experiments.

Harris said:

"If you never try a new thing, how can you tell what it's like? It's men such as you that hamper the world's progress. Think of the man who first tried German sausage!"

It was a great success, that Irish stew. I don't think I ever enjoyed a meal more. There was something so fresh and piquant about it. One's palate gets so tired of the old hackneyed things: here was a dish with a new flavour, with a taste like nothing else on earth.

And it was nourishing, too. As George said, there was good stuff in it. The peas and potatoes might have been a bit softer, but we all had good teeth, so that did not matter much: and as for the gravy, it was a poem - a little too rich, perhaps, for a weak stomach, but nutritious.

We finished up with tea and cherry tart. Montmorency had a fight with the kettle during tea-time, and came off a poor second.

Throughout the trip, he had manifested great curiosity concerning the kettle. He would sit and watch it, as it boiled, with a puzzled expression, and would try and rouse it every now and then by growling at it. When it began to splutter and steam, he regarded it as a challenge, and would want to fight it, only, at that precise moment, some one would always dash up and bear off his prey before he could get at it.

To-day he determined he would be beforehand. At the first sound the kettle made, he rose, growling, and advanced towards it in a threatening attitude. It was only a little kettle, but it was full of pluck, and it up and spit at him.

"Ah! would ye!" growled Montmorency, showing his teeth; "I'll teach ye to cheek a hard-working, respectable dog; ye miserable, long-nosed, dirty-looking scoundrel, ye. Come on!"

And he rushed at that poor little kettle, and seized it by the spout.

Then, across the evening stillness, broke a blood-curdling yelp, and Montmorency left the boat, and did a constitutional three times round the island at the rate of thirty-five miles an hour, stopping every now and then to bury his nose in a bit of cool mud.

From that day Montmorency regarded the kettle with a mixture of awe, suspicion, and hate. Whenever he saw it he would growl and back at a rapid rate, with his tail shut down, and the moment it was put upon the stove he would promptly climb out of the boat, and sit on the bank, till the whole tea business was over.

I slept well that night, and should have slept better if it had not been for Harris. I have a vague recollection of having been woke up at least a dozen times during the night by Harris wandering about the boat with the lantern, looking for his clothes. He seemed to be worrying about his clothes all night.

Twice he routed up George and myself to see if we were lying on his trousers. George got quite wild the second time.

"What the thunder do you want your trousers for, in the middle of the night?" he asked indignantly. "Why don't you lie down, and go to sleep?"

I found him in trouble, the next time I awoke, because he could not find his socks; and my last hazy remembrance is of being rolled over on my side, and of hearing Harris muttering something about its being an extraordinary thing where his umbrella could have got to.

❒

Chapter 8

George and Harris Shirk Their Work

We woke late the next morning, and, at Harris's earnest desire, partook of a plain breakfast, with "non dainties." Then we cleaned up, and put everything straight (a continual labour, which was beginning to afford me a pretty clear insight into a question that had often posed me - namely, how a woman with the work of only one house on her hands manages to pass away her time), and, at about ten, set out on what we had determined should be a good day's journey.

We agreed that we would pull this morning, as a change from towing; and Harris thought the best arrangement would be that George and I should scull, and he steer. I did not chime in with this idea at all; I said I thought Harris would have been showing a more proper spirit if he had suggested that he and George should work, and let me rest a bit. It seemed to me that I was doing more than my fair share of the work on this trip, and I was beginning to feel strongly on the subject.

It always does seem to me that I am doing more work than I should do. It is not that I object to the work, mind you; I like work: it fascinates me. I can sit and look at it for hours. I love to keep it by me: the idea of getting rid of it nearly breaks my heart.

You cannot give me too much work; to accumulate work has almost become a passion with me: my study is so full of it now, that there is hardly an inch of room for any more. I shall have to throw out a wing soon.

And I am careful of my work, too. Why, some of the work that I have by me now has been in my possession for years and years, and there isn't a finger-mark on it. I take a great pride in my work; I take it down now and then and dust it. No man keeps his work in a better state of preservation than I do.

But, though I crave for work, I still like to be fair. I do not ask for more than my proper share.

But I get it without asking for it - at least, so it appears to me - and this worries me.

George says he does not think I need trouble myself on the subject. He thinks it is only my over-scrupulous nature that makes me fear I am having more than my due; and that, as a matter of fact, I don't have half as much as I ought. But I expect he only says this to comfort me.

In a boat, I have always noticed that it is the fixed idea of each member of the crew that he is doing everything. Harris's notion was, that it was he alone who had been working, and that both George and I had been imposing upon him. George, on the other hand, ridiculed the idea of Harris's having done anything more than eat and sleep, and had a cast-iron opinion that it was he - George himself - who had done all the labour worth speaking of.

He said he had never been out with such a couple of lazily skulks as Harris and I.

That amused Harris.

"Fancy old George talking about work!" he laughed;

"why, about half-an-hour of it would kill him. Have you ever seen George work?" he added, turning to me.

I agreed with Harris that I never had - most certainly not since we had started on this trip.

"Well, I don't see how *you* can know much about it, one way or the other," George retorted on Harris; "for I'm blest if you haven't been asleep half the time. Have you ever seen Harris fully awake, except at meal-time?" asked George, addressing me.

Truth compelled me to support George. Harris had been very little good in the boat, so far as helping was concerned, from the beginning.

"Well, hang it all, I've done more than old J., anyhow," rejoined Harris.

"Well, you couldn't very well have done less," added George.

"I suppose J. thinks he is the passenger," continued Harris.

And that was their gratitude to me for having brought them and their wretched old boat all the way up from Kingston, and for having superintended and managed everything for them, and taken care of them, and slaved for them. It is the way of the world.

We settled the present difficulty by arranging that Harris and George should scull up past Reading, and that I should tow the boat on from there. Pulling a heavy boat against a strong stream has few attractions for me now. There was a time, long ago, when I used to clamour for the hard work: now I like to give the youngsters a chance.

I notice that most of the old river hands are similarly retiring, whenever there is any stiff pulling to be done. You can always tell the old river hand by the way in which he stretches himself out upon the cushions at the bottom of the boat, and encourages the rowers by telling them anecdotes about the marvellous feats he performed last season.

We came in sight of Reading about eleven. The river is dirty and dismal here. One does not linger in the neighbourhood of Reading. The town itself is a famous old place, dating from the dim days of King Ethelred, when the Danes anchored their warships in the Kennet, and started from Reading to ravage all the land of Wessex; and here Ethelred and his brother Alfred fought and defeated them, Ethelred doing the praying and Alfred the fighting.

In later years, Reading seems to have been regarded as a handy place to run down to, when matters were becoming unpleasant in London. Parliament generally rushed off to Reading whenever there was a plague on at Westminster; and, in 1625, the Law followed suit, and all the courts were held at Reading. It must have been worth while having a mere ordinary plague now and then in London to get rid of both the lawyers and the Parliament.

During the Parliamentary struggle, Reading was besieged by the Earl of Essex, and, a quarter of a century later, the Prince of Orange routed King James's troops there.

Henry I. lies buried at Reading, in the Benedictine abbey founded by him there, the ruins of which may still be seen; and, in this same abbey, great John of Gaunt was married to the Lady Blanche.

At Reading lock we came up with a steam launch, belonging to some friends of mine, and they towed us up to within about a mile of Streatley. It is very

The river becomes very lovely from a little above Reading.

delightful being towed up by a launch. I prefer it myself to rowing. The run would have been more delightful still, if it had not been for a lot of wretched small boats that were continually getting in the way of our launch, and, to avoid running down which, we had to be continually easing and stopping. It is really most annoying, the manner in which these rowing boats get in the way of one's launch up the river; something ought to done to stop it.

And they are so confoundedly impertinent, too, over it. You can whistle till you nearly burst your boiler before they will trouble themselves to hurry. I would have one or two of them run down now and then, if I had my way, just to teach them all a lesson.

The river becomes very lovely from a little above Reading. The railway rather spoils it near Tilehurst, but from Mapledurham up to Streatley it is glorious. A little above Mapledurham lock you pass Hardwick House, where Charles I. played bowls. The neighbourhood of Pangbourne, where the quaint little Swan Inn stands, must be as familiar to the *habitués* of the Art Exhibitions as it is to its own inhabitants.

My friends' launch cast us loose just below the grotto, and then Harris wanted to make out that it was my turn to pull. This seemed to me most unreasonable. It had been arranged in the morning that I should bring the boat up to three miles above Reading. Well, here we were, ten miles above Reading! Surely it was now their turn again.

I could not get either George or Harris to see the matter in its proper light, however; so, to save argument, I took the sculls. I had not been pulling for more than a minute or so, when George noticed something black floating on the water, and we drew up to it. George leant over, as we neared it, and laid hold of it. And then he drew back with a cry, and a blanched face.

It was the dead body of a woman. It lay very lightly on the water, and the face was sweet and calm. It was not a beautiful face; it was too prematurely aged-looking, too thin and drawn, to be that; but it was a gentle, lovable face, in spite of its stamp of pinch and poverty, and upon it was that look of restful peace that comes to the faces of the sick sometimes when at last the pain has left them.

Fortunately for us - we having no desire to be kept hanging about coroners' courts - some men on the bank had seen the body too, and now took charge of it from us.

We found out the woman's story afterwards. Of course it was the old, old vulgar tragedy. She had loved and been deceived - or had deceived herself. Anyhow, she had sinned - some of us do now and then - and her family and friends, naturally shocked and indignant, had closed their doors against her.

Left to fight the world alone, with the millstone of her shame around her neck, she had sunk ever lower and lower.

For a while she had kept both herself and the child on the twelve shillings a week that twelve hours' drudgery a day procured her, paying six shillings out of it for the child, and keeping her own body and soul together on the remainder.

Six shillings a week does not keep body and soul together very unitedly. They want to get away from each other when there is only such a very slight bond as that between them; and one day, I suppose, the pain and the dull monotony of it all had stood before her eyes plainer than usual, and the mocking spectre had frightened her. She had made one last appeal to friends, but, against the chill wall of their respectability, the voice of the erring outcast fell unheeded; and then she had gone to see her child - had held it in her arms and kissed it, in a weary, dull sort of way, and without betraying any particular emotion of any kind, and had left it, after putting into its hand a penny box of chocolate she had bought it, and afterwards, with her last few shillings, had taken a ticket and come down to Goring.

It seemed that the bitterest thoughts of her life must have centred about the wooded reaches and the bright green meadows around Goring; but women strangely hug the knife that stabs them, and, perhaps, amidst the gall, there may have mingled also sunny memories of sweetest hours, spent upon those shadowed deeps over which the great trees bend their branches down so low.

She had wandered about the woods by the river's brink all day, and then, when evening fell and the grey twilight spread its dusky robe upon the waters, she stretched her arms out to the silent river that had known her sorrow and her joy. And the old river had taken her into its gentle arms, and had laid her weary head upon its bosom, and had hushed away the pain.

Thus had she sinned in all things - sinned in living and in dying. God help her! and all other sinners, if any more there be.

Goring on the left bank and Streatley on the right are both or either charming places to stay at for a few days. The reaches down to Pangbourne woo one for a sunny sail or for a moonlight row, and the country round about is full of beauty. We had intended to push on to Wallingford that day, but the sweet smiling face of the river here lured us to linger for a while; and so we left our boat at the bridge, and went up into Streatley, and lunched at the "Bull," much to Montmorency's satisfaction.

They say that the hills on each ride of the stream here once joined and formed a barrier across what is now the Thames, and that then the river ended there above Goring in one vast lake. I am not in a position either to contradict or affirm this statement. I simply offer it.

It is an ancient place, Streatley, dating back, like most river-side towns and villages, to British and Saxon times. Goring is not nearly so pretty a little spot to stop at as Streatley, if you have your choice; but it is passing fair enough in its way, and is nearer the railway in case you want to slip off without paying your hotel bill.

❐

Chapter 9

The Astonishing Trout

We stayed two days at Streatley, and got our clothes washed. We had tried washing them ourselves, in the river, under George's superintendence, and it had been a failure. Indeed, it had been more than a failure, because we were worse off after we had washed our clothes than we were before. Before we had washed them, they had been very, very dirty, it is true; but they were just wearable. *After* we had washed them - well, the river between Reading and Henley was much cleaner, after we had washed our clothes in it, than it was before. All the dirt contained in the river between Reading and Henley, we collected, during that wash, and worked it into our clothes.

The washerwoman at Streatley said she felt she owed it to herself to charge us just three times the usual prices for that wash. She said it had not been like washing, it had been more in the nature of excavating.

We paid the bill without a murmur.

The neighbourhood of Streatley and Goring is a great fishing centre. There is some excellent fishing to be had here. The river abounds in pike, roach, dace, gudgeon, and eels, just here; and you can sit and fish for them all day.

Some people do. They never catch them. I never knew anybody catch anything, up the Thames, except minnows and dead cats, but that has nothing to do, of course, with fishing! The local fisherman's guide doesn't say a word about catching anything. All it says is the place is "a good station for fishing;" and, from what I have seen of the district, I am quite prepared to bear out this statement.

There is no spot in the world where you can get more fishing, or where you can fish for a longer period. Some fishermen come here and fish for a day, and others stop and fish for a month. You can hang on and fish for a year, if you want to: it will be all the same.

The *Angler's Guide to the Thames* says that "jack and perch are also to be had about here," but there the *Angler's Guide* is wrong. Jack and perch may *be* about there. Indeed, I know for a fact that they are. You can *see* them there in shoals, when you are out for a walk along the banks: they come and stand half out of the water with their mouths open for biscuits. And, if you go for a bathe, they crowd round, and get in your way, and irritate you. But they are not to be "had" by a bit of worm on the end of a hook, nor anything like it - not they!

I am not a good fisherman myself. I devoted a considerable amount of attention to the subject at one time, and was getting on, as I thought, fairly well; but the old hands told me that I should never be any real good at it, and advised me to give it up. They said that I was an extremely neat thrower, and that I seemed to have plenty of gumption for the thing, and quite enough constitutional laziness. But they were sure I should never make anything of a fisherman. I had not got sufficient imagination.

They said that as a poet, or a shilling shocker, or a reporter, or anything of that kind, I might be satisfactory, but that, to gain any position as a Thames angler, would require more play of fancy, more power of invention than I appeared to possess.

Some people are under the impression that all that is required to make a good fisherman is the ability to tell lies easily and without blushing; but this is a mistake. Mere bald fabrication is useless; the veriest tyro can manage that. It is in the circumstantial detail, the embellishing touches of probability, the general air of scrupulous - almost of pedantic - veracity, that the experienced angler is seen.

Anybody can come in and say, "Oh, I caught fifteen dozen perch yesterday evening;" or "Last Monday I landed a gudgeon, weighing eighteen pounds, and measuring three feet from the tip to the tail."

There is no art, no skill, required for that sort of thing. It shows pluck, but that is all.

No; your accomplished angler would scorn to tell a lie, that way. His method is a study in itself.

He comes in quietly with his hat on, appropriates the most comfortable chair, lights his pipe, and commences to puff in silence. He lets the youngsters brag away for a while, and then, during a momentary lull, he removes the pipe from his mouth, and remarks, as he knocks the ashes out against the bars:

"Well, I had a haul on Tuesday evening that it's not much good my telling anybody about."

"Oh! why's that?" they ask.

"Because I don't expect anybody would believe me if I did," replies the old fellow calmly, and without

"No," he continues thoughtfully.

even a tinge of bitterness in his tone, as he refills his pipe, and requests the landlord to bring him three of Scotch, cold.

There is a pause after this, nobody feeling sufficiently sure of himself to contradict the old gentleman. So he has to go on by himself without any encouragement.

"No," he continues thoughtfully; "I shouldn't believe it myself if anybody told it to me, but it's a fact, for all that. I had been sitting there all the afternoon and had caught literally nothing - except a few dozen dace and a score of jack; and I was just about giving it up as a bad job when I suddenly felt a rather smart pull at the line. I thought it was another little one, and I went to jerk it up. Hang me, if I could move the rod! It took me half-an-hour - half-an-hour, sir! - to land that fish; and every moment I thought the line was going to snap! I reached him at last, and what do you think it was? A sturgeon! a forty pound sturgeon! taken on a line, sir! Yes, you may well look surprised - I'll have another three of Scotch, landlord, please."

And then he goes on to tell of the astonishment of everybody who saw it; and what his wife said, when he got home, and of what Joe Buggles thought about it.

I asked the landlord of an inn up the river once, if it did not injure him, sometimes, listening to the tales that the fishermen about there told him; and he said:

"Oh, no; not now, sir. It did used to knock me over a bit at first, but, lor love you! me and the missus we listens to 'em all day now. It's what you're used to, you know. It's what you're used to."

George and I - I don't know what had become of Harris; he had gone out and had a shave, early in the afternoon, and had then come back and spent full forty minutes in pipeclaying his shoes, we had not seen him since - George and I, therefore, and the dog, left to ourselves, went for a walk to Wallingford on the second evening, and, coming home, we called in at a little river-side inn, for a rest, and other things.

We went into the parlour and sat down. There was an old fellow there, smoking a long clay pipe, and we naturally began chatting.

He told us that it had been a fine day to-day, and we told him that it had been a fine day yesterday, and then we all told each other that we thought it would be a fine day to-morrow; and George said the crops seemed to be coming up nicely.

After that it came out, somehow or other, that we were strangers in the neighbourhood, and that we were going away the next morning.

Then a pause ensued in the conversation, during which our eyes wandered round the room. They finally rested upon a dusty old glass-case, fixed very high up above the chimney-piece, and containing a trout. It rather fascinated me, that trout; it was such a monstrous fish. In fact, at first glance, I thought it was a cod.

"Ah!" said the old gentleman, following the direction of my gaze, "fine fellow that, ain't he?"

"Quite uncommon," I murmured; and George asked the old man how much he thought it weighed.

"Eighteen pounds six ounces," said our friend, rising and taking down his coat. "Yes," he continued, "it wur sixteen year ago, come the third o' next month, that I landed him. I caught him just below the bridge with a minnow. They told me he wur in the river, and I said I'd have him, and so I did. You don't see many fish that size about here now, I'm thinking. Good-night, gentlemen, good-night."

And out he went, and left us alone.

We could not take our eyes off the fish after that. It really was a remarkably fine fish. We were still looking at it, when the local carrier, who had just stopped at the inn, came to the door of the room with a pot of beer in his hand, and he also looked at the fish.

And then he told us the real history of the fish. It seemed that he had caught it himself, years ago, when he was quite a lad; not by any art or skill, but by that unaccountable luck that appears to always wait upon a boy when he plays the wag from school, and goes out fishing on a sunny afternoon, with a bit of string tied on to the end of a tree.

He said that bringing home that trout had saved him from a whacking, and that even his school-master had said it was worth the rule-of-three and practice put together.

He was called out of the room at this point, and George and I again turned our gaze upon the fish.

It really was a most astonishing trout. The more we looked at it, the more we marvelled at it.

It excited George so much that he climbed up on the back of a chair to get a better view of it.

And then the chair slipped, and George clutched wildly at the trout-case to save himself, and down it came with a crash, George and the chair on top of it.

"You haven't injured the fish, have you?" I cried in alarm, rushing up.

"I hope not," said George, rising cautiously and looking about.

But he had. That trout lay shattered into a thousand

fragments - I say a thousand, but they may have only been nine hundred. I did not count them.

We thought it strange and unaccountable that a stuffed trout should break up into little pieces like that.

And so it would have been strange and unaccountable, if it had been a stuffed trout, but it was not.

That trout was plaster-of-Paris.

We left Streatley early the next morning, and pulled up to Culham, and slept under the canvas, in the backwater there.

The river is not extraordinarily interesting between Streatley and Wallingford. From Cleve you get a stretch of six and a half miles without a lock. I believe this is the longest uninterrupted stretch anywhere above Teddington, and the Oxford Club make use of it for their trial eights.

But however satisfactory this absence of locks may be to rowing-men, it is to be regretted by the mere pleasure-seeker.

For myself, I am fond of locks. They pleasantly break the monotony of the pull. I like sitting in the boat and slowly rising out of the cool depths up into new reaches and fresh views; or sinking down, as it were, out of the world, and then waiting, while the gloomy gates creak, and the narrow strip of day-light between them widens till the fair smiling river lies full before you, and you push your little boat out from its brief prison on to the welcoming waters once again.

They are picturesque little spots, these locks. The stout old lock-keeper, or his cheerful-looking wife, or bright-eyed daughter, are pleasant folk to have a passing chat with.* You meet other boats there, and river gossip is exchanged. The Thames would not be the fairyland it is without its flower-decked locks.

* Or rather *were*. The Conservancy of late seems to have constituted itself into a society for the employment of idiots. A good many of the new lock-keepers, especially in the more crowded portions of the river, are excitable, nervous old men, quite unfitted for their post.

Talking of locks reminds me of an accident George and I very nearly had one summer's morning at Hampton Court.

It was a glorious day, and the Lock was crowded; and, as is a common practice up the river, a speculative photographer was taking a picture of us all as we lay upon the rising waters.

I did not catch what was going on at first, and was, therefore, extremely surprised at noticing George hurriedly smooth out his trousers, ruffle up his hair, and stick his cap on in a rakish manner at the back of his head, and then, assuming an expression of mingled affability and sadness, sit down in a graceful attitude, and try to hide his feet.

My first idea was that he had suddenly caught sight of some girl he knew, and I looked about to see who it was. Everybody in the lock seemed to have been suddenly struck wooden. They were all standing or sitting about in the most quaint and curious attitudes I have ever seen off a Japanese fan. All the girls were smiling. Oh, they did look so sweet! And all the fellows were frowning, and looking stern and noble.

And then, at last, the truth flashed across me, and I wondered if I should be in time. Ours was the first boat, and it would be unkind of me to spoil the man's picture, I thought.

So I faced round quickly, and took up a position in the prow, where I leant with careless grace upon the hitcher, in an attitude suggestive of agility and strength. I arranged my hair with a curl over the forehead, and threw an air of tender wistfulness into my expression, mingled with a touch of cynicism, which I am told suits me.

As we stood, waiting for the eventful moment, I heard someone behind call out:

"Hi! look at your nose."

I could not turn round to see what was the matter, and whose nose it was that was to be looked at. I stole a side-glance at George's nose! It was all right - at all events, there was nothing wrong with it that could be altered. I squinted down at my own, and that seemed all that could be expected also.

"Look at your nose, you stupid ass!" came the same voice again, louder.

And then another voice cried:

"Push your nose out, can't you, you - you two with the dog!"

Neither George nor I dared to turn round. The man's hand was on the cap, and the picture might be taken any moment. Was it us they were calling to? What was the matter with our noses? Why were they to be pushed out!

But now the whole lock started yelling, and a stentorian voice from the back shouted:

"Look at your boat, sir; you in the red and black caps. It's your two corpses that will get taken in that photo, if you ain't quick."

We looked then, and saw that the nose of our boat had got fixed under the woodwork of the lock, while the in-coming water was rising all around it, and tilting it up. In another moment we should be over. Quick as thought, we each seized an oar, and a vigorous blow against the side of the lock with the butt-ends released the boat, and sent us sprawling on our backs.

We did not come out well in that photograph, George and I. Of course, as was to be expected, our luck ordained it, that the man should set his wretched machine in motion at the precise moment that we were both lying on our backs with a wild expression of "Where am I? and what is it?" on our faces, and our four feet waving madly in the air.

Our feet were undoubtedly the leading article in that photograph. Indeed, very little else was to be seen. They filled up the foreground entirely. Behind them, you caught glimpses of the other boats, and bits of the surrounding scenery; but everything and everybody else in the lock looked so utterly insignificant and paltry compared with our feet, that all the other people felt quite ashamed of themselves, and refused to subscribe to the picture.

The owner of one steam launch, who had bespoke six copies, rescinded the order on seeing the negative. He said he would take them if anybody could show him his launch, but nobody could. It was somewhere behind George's right foot.

There was a good deal of unpleasantness over the business. The photographer thought we ought to take a dozen copies each, seeing that the photo was about nine-tenths us, but we declined. We said we had no objection to being photo'd full-length, but we preferred being taken the right way up.

We were up early the next morning, as we wanted to be in Oxford by the afternoon. It is surprising how early one can get up, when camping out. One does not yearn for "just another five minutes" nearly so much, lying wrapped up in a rug on the boards of a boat, with a Gladstone bag for a pillow, as one does in a featherbed. We had finished breakfast, and were through Clifton Lock by half-past eight.

From Clifton to Culham the river banks are flat, monotonous, and uninteresting, but, after you have got through Culhalm Lock - the coldest and deepest lock on the river - the landscape improves.

❐

Chapter 10

Back Home

We spent two very pleasant days at Oxford. There are plenty of dogs in the town of Oxford. Montmorency had eleven fights on the first day, and fourteen on the second, and evidently thought he had got to heaven.

Among folk too constitutionally weak, or too constitutionally lazy, whichever it may be, to relish up-stream work, it is a common practice to get a boat at Oxford, and row down. For the energetic, however, the up-stream journey is certainly to be preferred. It does not seem good to be always going with the current. There is more satisfaction in squaring one's back, and fighting against it, and winning one's way forward in spite of it - at least, so I feel, when Harris and George are sculling and I am steering.

The neighbourhood of the upper Thames is rich in Roman relics, and my surmise seemed to me a very probable one; but our serious young man, who is a bit of a geologist, pooh-poohed my Roman relic theory, and said it was clear to the meanest intellect (in which category he seemed to be grieved that he could not conscientiously include mine) that the thing the boy had found was the fossil of a whale; and he pointed out to us various evidences proving that it must have belonged to the preglacial period.

To settle the dispute, we appealed to the boy. We

told him not to be afraid, but to speak the plain truth: Was it the fossil of a pre-Adamite whale, or was it an early Roman coffin?

The boy said it was *The Pride of the Thames.*

We thought this a very humorous answer on the part of the boy at first, and somebody gave him twopence as a reward for his ready wit; but when he persisted in keeping up the joke, as we thought, too long, we got vexed with him.

"Come, come, my lad!" said our captain sharply, "don't let us have any nonsense. You take your mother's washing-tub home again, and bring us a boat."

The boat-builder himself came up then, and assured us, on his word, as a practical man, that the thing really was a boat - was, in fact, *the* boat, the "double sculling skiff" selected to take us on our trip down the river.

We grumbled a good deal. We thought he might, at least, have had it whitewashed or tarred - had *something* done to it to distinguish it from a bit of a wreck; but he could not see any fault in it.

He even seemed offended at our remarks. He said he had picked us out the best boat in all his stock, and he thought we might have been more grateful.

He said it, *The Pride of the Thames,* had been in use, just as it now stood (or rather as it now hung together), for the last forty years, to his knowledge, and nobody had complained of it before, and he did not see why we should be the first to begin.

We argued no more.

We fastened the so-called boat together with some pieces of string, got a bit of wall-paper and pasted over the shabbier places, said our prayers, and stepped on board.

They charged us thirty-five shillings for the loan of the remnant for six days; and we could have bought the thing out-and-out for four-and-sixpence at any sale of drift-wood round the coast.

Sunlight is the life-blood of Nature. Mother Earth looks at us with such dull, soulless eyes, when the sunlight has died away from out of her. It makes us sad to be with her then; she does not seem to know us or to care for us. She is as a widow who has lost the husband she loved, and her children touch her hand, and look up into her eyes, but gain no smile from her.

We rowed on all that day through the rain, and very melancholy work it was. We pretended, at first, that we enjoyed it. We said it was a change, and that we liked to see the river under all its different aspects. We said we could not expect to have it all sunshine, nor should we wish it. We told each other that Nature was beautiful, even in her tears.

Indeed, Harris and I were quite enthusiastic about the business, for the first few hours. And we sang a song about a gipsy's life, and how delightful a gipsy's existence was! - free to storm and sunshine, and to every wind that blew! - and how he enjoyed the rain, and what a lot of good it did him; and how he laughed at people who didn't like it.

George took the fun more soberly, and stuck to the umbrella.

We hoisted the cover before we had lunch, and kept it up all the afternoon, just leaving a little space in the bow, from which one of us could paddle and keep a look-out. In this way we made nine miles, and pulled up for the night a little below Day's Lock.

I cannot honestly say that we had a merry evening.

George requested that we would not talk about these things.

The rain poured down with quiet persistency. Everything in the boat was damp and clammy. Supper was not a success. Cold veal pie, when you don't feel hungry, is apt to cloy. I felt I wanted whitebait and a cutlet; Harris babbled of soles and white-sauce, and passed the remains of his pie to Montmorency, who declined it, and, apparently insulted by the offer, went and sat over at the other end of the boat by himself.

George requested that we would not talk about these things, at all events until he had finished his cold boiled beef without mustard.

We played penny nap after supper. We played for about an hour and a half, by the end of which time George had won fourpence - George always is lucky at cards - and Harris and I had lost exactly twopence each.

We thought we would give up gambling then. As Harris said, it breeds an unhealthy excitement when carried too far. George offered to go on and give us our revenge; but Harris and I decided not to battle any further against Fate.

After that, we mixed ourselves some toddy, and sat round and talked. George told us about a man he had known, who had come up the river two years ago and who had slept out in a damp boat on just such another night as that was, and it had given him rheumatic fever, and nothing was able to save him, and he had died in great agony ten days afterwards. George said he was quite a young man, and was engaged to be married. He said it was one of the saddest things he had ever known.

We should be in at Pangbourne by five. We should finish dinner at, say, half-past six. After that we could walk about the village in the pouring rain until bed-time; or we could sit in a dimly-lit bar-parlour and read the almanac.

"Why, the Alhambra would be almost more lively," said Harris, venturing his head outside the cover for a moment and taking a survey of the sky.

"Yes it's almost a pity we've made up our minds to stick to this boat," answered Harris; and then there was silence for a while.

We reached Paddington at seven, and drove direct to the restaurant I have before described, where we partook of a light meal, left Montmorency, together with suggestions for a supper to be ready at half-past ten, and then continued our way to Leicester Square.

We attracted a good deal of attention at the Alhambra. On our presenting ourselves at the paybox we were gruffly directed to go round to Castle Street, and were informed that we were half-an-hour behind our time.

We convinced the man, with some difficulty, that we were not "the world-renowned contortionists from the Himalaya Mountains," and he took our money and let us pass.

Inside we were a still greater success. Our fine bronzed countenances and picturesque clothes were followed round the place with admiring gaze. We were the cynosure of every eye.

It was a proud moment for us all.

We adjourned soon after the first ballet, and wended our way back to the restaurant, where supper was already awaiting us.

"Well," said Harris, reaching his hand out for his glass, "we have had a pleasant trip, and my hearty thanks for it to old Father Thames - but I think we did well to chuck it when we did. Here's to Three Men well out of a Boat!"

Hearing the words of Harris Montmorency peeped out of the window and gave out a hearty bark to announce his happiness.

❒

Questions Based on the Story

Chapter1

Three Men Plan Their Journey

Q.1 Name the three men who decided to go on a boating holiday.

Q.2 What was the name of the dog which accompanied the three men?

Chapter 2

Discussing the Things

Q.1 When Aunt Podger would ask what was to be done with the photo-frame, What was uncle Podger's reply?

Q.2 What did George suggest for other breakfast things?

Chapter 3

On Their Way

Q.1 Whom had Montmorency invited to see him off?

Q.2 How did the quaint back-streets of Kingston look in the flashing sunlight?

Chapter 4

At the River-bank

Q.1 What did the two girls do before they sat in the boat?

Q.2 In the evening, where did all the three men visit? How did they enjoy themselves there?

Chapter 5

First Night Under Canvas

Q.1 What did Harris say to George as regards work?

Q.2 How did the three men behave before and after supper?

Chapter 6

An Angel Comes By

Q.1 What amusing thing happened with the narrator while dressing one morning?

Q.2 Why did Harris not like the look of the man who was learning against the front door?

Chapter 7

Fight Between Montmorency and Tea-Kettle

Q.1 Give the description of Marlow.

Q.2 What seemed a fascinating idea to all the three men ?

Chapter 8

George and Harris Shirk Their Work

Q.1 Why did Reading come to be considered as a handy place in later years ?

Q.2 Whose dead body was it, which George laid hold of in the water?

Chapter 9

The Astonishing Trout

Q.1 Why was the trout an astonishing fish?

Q.2 What did the owner of the steam-launch do on seeing the negative?

Chapter 10

Back Home

Q.1 How many fights had Montmorency on the first and second days?

Q.2 When did they all reach Paddington and how did they attract a good deal of attention at the Alhambra?

❑❑❑